MILD VERTIGO

MIEKO KANAI

Mild Vertigo

translated from the Japanese
by Polly Barton

with an afterword
by Kate Zambreno

A NEW DIRECTIONS PAPERBOOK ORIGINAL

First Japanese edition published as *Karui Memai* in 1997 by Kodansha Ltd.,
Tokyo. Publication rights for this English edition arranged through
Kodansha Ltd.

New Directions gratefully acknowledges the support of JAPANFOUNDATION.

Manufactured in the United States of America
First published as a New Directions Paperbook (NDP1562) in 2023

Library of Congress Cataloging-in-Publication Data
Names: Kanai, Mieko, 1947- author. | Barton, Polly, translator. |
Zambreno, Kate, writer of afterword.
Title: Mild vertigo / Mieko Kanai ; translated by Polly Barton ;
afterword by Kate Zambreno.
Other titles: Karui Memai. English
Description: New York : New Directions Publishing Corporation, 2023.
Identifiers: LCCN 2023001717 | ISBN 9780811232289 (paperback ;
acid-free paper) | ISBN 9780811232296 (ebook)
Subjects: LCGFT: Novels.
Classification: LCC PL855.A52 K3713 2023 | DDC 895.63/5--dc23/eng/20230208
LC record available at https://lccn.loc.gov/2023001717

10 9 8 7 6 5 4 3 2

New Directions Books are published for James Laughlin
by New Directions Publishing Corporation
80 Eighth Avenue, New York 10011

Chapter One – Tap Water

THE REASON THEY'D SETTLED on that apartment with its large, open-plan kitchen and windows with sizable balconies to both the south and east sides wasn't any particular passion for cooking on Natsumi's part, let alone any special pride she took in her culinary abilities, but because it looked like the interiors she often saw and admired in the glossy pages of women's magazines, and it had a kitchen island with a breakfast bar, as was now all the rage, or in vogue, or whatever you wanted to call it, which seemed like a pretty convenient feature, and above anything else, the front door of the two-bedroom apartment they'd been living in until that point, which hadn't been a new build or anything, opened directly into the kitchen, so when you walked in you were immediately confronted by the sight of the sink and the gas stove and the fridge, and her mother, who'd never lived in either public housing or any other kind of apartment complex, would always comment that you shouldn't open up the front door of the apartment and be right inside the kitchen, it makes the whole place feel impoverished, and honestly, if you don't keep the sink spick and span then it'll look even more impoverished, this became a catchphrase of hers every time she came over, and then she'd

1

go on to say, I don't care how cheap the mortgage payments are here, I just think an apartment with a separate kitchen would make things much easier, because as a housewife, you're in there every day, she'd point out, darting glances at the sink and the stove, which of course weren't kept in as pristine a state as Natsumi would ideally have liked, whereas in this new apartment with its breakfast bar, the front door didn't open directly onto the kitchen, there was instead a proper vestibule, even if it was slightly cramped, which led to a hall, and a door with glass panels framed in white wood separating the hall from the main living space, which meant you could avoid having visitors unexpectedly catching a glimpse of your chaotically messy kitchen in its entirety, which she preferred, and in terms of the size of the apartment—the open-plan room was about twelve tatami mats large, and then there was a six-mat room with tatami flooring, a three-mat utility room off the kitchen, and two rooms, eight mats and seven mats in size, with Western-style flooring—she couldn't help but feel it was somewhat luxuriously spacious for a family like hers, composed of herself and her husband and two children of kindergarten and elementary school age, and the kids were very excited about the children's pool in the courtyard of the new apartment block, and even though it was really only big enough to splash around in and not to actually swim laps, they declared it soooo cool, we'll be like rich people, they said, and although it was blindingly obvious to Natsumi that they'd get sick of the pool in no time and it would become an object of ridicule, for the moment they were over the moon, and though the eight-mat room was currently being used by her husband as his "study," she figured that when the kids moved up to middle school they'd probably grow dissatisfied with the current arrangement, which had them sleeping in bunk beds in the seven-mat room, and they'd want their "own rooms," and if that happened, then they could free up the "study" and move one of the kids in there, and her husband could use the utility room—which currently accommodated a washing machine, tumble dryer, and laundry basket, and then, on the opposite wall, a lightweight wall-storage unit they'd ordered online made of white-polyester-resin-coated plywood, which fit the dimensions of the room as snugly as if it'd been made to measure—as his "study" instead, at least that was what they'd discussed, but if that situation actually materialized, she had no idea where on earth they'd put the washing machine, or the tumble dryer, or the storage unit—which was used for the vacuum and the washing and cleaning products, as well as canned goods and other food supplies she'd bought in reserve, and various odds and ends in assorted shapes and sizes—and, to add to their problems, the "study" currently contained five bookshelves made of steel and plywood, a desk, a computer, and a video camera, which her husband had been using as part of a project to "create a record of the family"—a project that, whether because he'd gotten fed up with filming or because he'd never really had much in the way of a visual sensibility to begin with, he had subsequently abandoned, having shot not even ten hours of footage in total, a good portion of which had its subjects' heads lopped from the frame—as well as a chest expander he'd used back in his student days, and something called a Super Gym DX (made in Taiwan), which promised "Real Results from Everyday Training," offering "Training as Good as You'd Get in Any Gym, Thanks to a Hydraulic Cylinder, for Convenient Home Workouts Whenever Suits You! Cure a Lack of Exercise, Tone and Shape Up and Improve Strength," and which he'd bought without consulting her, and though it hadn't been all that expensive, it weighed sixty-six pounds and two ounces and was three feet and nine inches wide, five feet and three inches deep, and four feet and ten inches tall, and when she thought about all these things she felt like taking them out with the trash tomorrow and being done with it, but in any case, it wouldn't be for another five or six years that they'd have to consider making these new arrangements, and now as she was trying to figure things out, to make calculations involving the layout of the apartment and the furniture, which should in theory have been simple, there was always some kind of slip-up involved (when she finally thought she'd solved the issue so that everything would fit, it would turn out that the door in fact opened into the room, even though logically it should have opened out, and so on), and, deciding that worrying too much about these kinds of things was ultimately detrimental, she resolved to stop obsessing over them. I guess we can figure it out in due course, right, she said to her husband, and he replied from where he was lying sprawled out on the sofa, his head propped up on a pile of cushions, not removing his gaze from the TV screen, right, right, all in due course, which irritated her slightly, but it wasn't like the issue was presenting a problem for her now in the present moment, in fact it really was true that they could just figure it out in due course, so she refrained from saying what she was tempted to say, which was, but that's what you always say.

Somehow the new kitchen in the new apartment seemed too good for her, which meant she rarely felt like making the most of it, and she was particularly reluctant to do anything along the lines of deep-frying, which would get those practically immaculate enamel and light-wood surfaces dirty, and although she felt that she was failing as a housewife and a mother in not doing so, she couldn't bring herself to make the sorts of meals that would mess up the kitchen.

And I mean, she ends up saying to her husband, what if I

were to make tempura at home? I'm talking about if I researched how to do it properly and managed to make tempura that was halfway decent, it still wouldn't be half as good as the stuff made by a tempura chef in a real tempura restaurant, would it? I was brought up in a simple, very ordinary sort of household by a mother who wasn't remotely well informed about food, and who didn't have any particular love of cooking, and now I'm just a regular housewife, not someone working at a tempura restaurant, and even if I did manage to pull it off, don't you think there's something so unsophisticated about going around bragging about the fact, saying to your friends and colleagues, ahh, you know, the tempura my wife makes is quite something, and all that kind of nonsense, I find it totally pathetic.

At which her husband, with whom this has clearly struck a chord, nods deeply and says, now that you say it, I feel like the guys who go around boasting about their wives' cooking are always the really wimpy ones, the kind of guy who was all skin and bones when he was younger, but begins to fill out in middle age until he ends up looking like a flabby old capybara, so that when he gets naked his dick, which was hardly anything to write home about to begin with, looks extra minuscule, he says, and regardless of whether or not it's true, he goes on to say, boasting about your wife's cooking is, when you think about it, a sign that you're totally under her thumb in an oral-fixation kind of a way, and you've made your relationship with her into a mother-and-child one, which is just such a cliché for Japanese men, right, he says, nodding, satisfied. The kids greet the ready-made katsu and tempura that she's bought at the supermarket and reheated in the microwave without complaint, and, of course, the way they eat those things is different from how they eat the meals she's prepared from scratch, which means they're capable of making those kinds of subtle distinctions when it comes to taste, or rather that they have the ability to judge whether something is good or not, and it seems to her that as long as you're providing your children with the types of food that get them to the point where they can form their own judgments in that way, then it's fine to slack off a bit sometimes, besides, eating deep-fried foods inevitably means consuming a lot of oil, and when you get too accustomed to the taste of fried food you end up finding anything else somehow lacking, and in a way it's a kind of addiction, just like smoking or alcohol or drugs, at least that's what she read in a magazine article about dieting, and of course it's also important for her husband's health that he eats well, and it's not good for the kids to have too much grease either, in the long term, which is the explanation she gives for why she doesn't cook oily food, and if that's contradicted by the pork katsu and croquettes and tempura and deep-fried chicken that she buys preprepared from the butcher or the supermarket and that sometimes shows up on their dinner table, it's not something that her husband or kids call her out on.

The apartment is in theory thirty minutes by bus from Shibuya, but of course it sometimes takes longer than that depending on traffic, and you can also get there by taking the Odakyu Line from Shinjuku to Chitose-Funabashi, then catching the bus from outside Chitose-Funabashi Station and getting off at Nodai-Mae, and from there it's a four- or five-minute walk, and it's a great neighborhood for children, with the Tokyo University of Agriculture campus and the Equestrian Park nearby, and of course it was reasonably priced, and even if they end up selling it someday and building their own house in Mejiro, where her parents live, they figure they'll at least have satisfied their desire to live somewhere a bit different (even if it's still Tokyo), which was their rationale for buying the place, and apparently it was put on the market because its previous owner was in sudden need of cash, and though at seven years old it wasn't exactly new it didn't feel like a relic either—whether the previous owner always knew they'd sell it someday or whether they were just the fussy type who enjoyed cleaning, there were barely any signs of wear and tear or stains or anything like that. The ready-made kitchen unit with its imitation-marble countertop and the large oven with built-in microwave could of course be used just as they were, and so the renovations they made were limited to switching the tatami matting in the six-mat room over to laminate flooring, replacing the Japanese-style sliding-door closet for a Western-style wardrobe, and the wallpaper in the seven-mat room had been French or something, with pink, light-blue, orange, and brown flowers sprinkled across a pale cream background in a rococo style, or whatever the right term is, she didn't know precisely what the style was called but in any case, it was an exaggeratedly romantic or perhaps just a "classic" floral print, and there was a chandelier-style lamp hanging from the ceiling that was presumably intended to match the wallpaper, with patterns etched into its frosted glass and twelve dangling crystal pendants shaped like teardrops, if we had girls, her husband had said, then maybe they'd take to it, pretend it was a princess's room, but there's just no way this can work as a boys' room, it's too weird, to which she replied, even if we did have girls I wouldn't want to make them live in a stupid, tasteless room like this, so they changed the wallpaper to one of a simple design and put in fluorescent lighting, and of course swapped the rose-pink carpet for laminate flooring, and although the older boy didn't really want to transfer to a new school, things panned out so that he started at his new school at the beginning of the school year in April, so that was easy enough, and the younger boy, who started kindergarten, took to it very quickly, and a year passed, in theory everything was going very well, and the fact that they'd changed the flooring—particularly in the kids' bedroom—to laminate meant that cleaning was simple, and it was also far more hygienic compared to carpet, which makes it easy for dust mites to multiply, and besides, laminate flooring is in fashion, so of course they were going to go for that, but where she suspects they might have messed up a little is in overlooking the fact that sound travels more easily to the floors below with laminate flooring, and the woman from the apartment directly beneath theirs—whose face she recognized because when they'd first moved in Natsumi had dropped by her apartment, as well as the other apartments directly adjacent and above, to present her neighbors with thousand-yen (excluding tax) boxes of rice crackers (containing three bags of three different kinds: plain, deep-fried arare with peanuts, and shinagawa maki, which she'd purchased after consulting her mother, who'd said that rice crackers were better in this situation than cookies, which people of the older generation might have reservations about)—had said to her, when they bumped into each other by the garbage collection point, you've got two boys, right, and aren't they ever so lively! I know people say that children these days are always studying, all they do is go to cram schools, and when they do have free time, they just sit inside playing their computer games, barely moving a muscle, but it seems they do move around when they're inside after all, don't they, which was clearly a barbed comment about how noisy her kids were, so she apologized out of embarrassment, but the comment stayed with her long afterward, because her kids don't go stomping around that much, and if the noise is nonetheless audible in the apartment downstairs then maybe there's some issue with the building itself—quite possibly the space between the floor and the ceiling below is too thin or not well insulated enough—which gave her the horrible feeling of having made an unwise purchase, and since it's obvious that carpet would be better at absorbing noise than laminate, maybe we should've gone for that, she says to her husband, to which he responds, roughly how old is this woman, and she replies somewhat vaguely, hmm, let's see, I'd put her somewhere between forty-seven or forty-eight and sixty-five, at which her husband says, it's understandable, when you're estimating someone's age, to say "around fifty" or something along those lines, but it's weird to put it like that, to say "somewhere between forty-seven or forty-eight and sixty-five." And if you want to know why it sounds weird, it's because using an age range of nearly twenty years is what they do when describing unidentified corpses, in fact in the paper this morning there was an article that said, the woman in question is five feet, two inches in height, with long, permed hair dyed light brown, wearing a pink sweater and an expensively tailored tight beige skirt, good-quality sandals in light and dark brown leather, with gold earrings, from her attire she's believed to be a high earner between twenty and forty years of age, and those are exactly the kinds of occasions when it's used, don't you think that's a weird thing to say about a living person, someone you've actually had a conversation with, that she's "somewhere between forty-seven or forty-eight and sixty-five"?

You only say that because you haven't actually met the woman downstairs, anyone who's seen her would describe her like I did, if she looked somewhere around fifty then I'd just say that, wouldn't I, but what I'm trying to say is she's a strange case, almost ageless, it's as though she misrepresents her age somehow, she said, and thus their conversation veered wildly off course, and in any case, when it came to the floor above them, it wasn't like they never heard a peep, of course if people are going about their lives then there's going to be at least some noise, like the toilet flushing in the middle of the night, the trickling and surging of water through the elaborate system of water and sewage pipes that runs through the entire building, and the burner for the eight-year-old gas boiler on their balcony that probably needs replacing, which the kids say sounds like a monster roaring, and the sound of slippered feet shuffling across the floor, and that of doors being opened and closed violently, but that's really it, and the children in the apartment above, a boy and a girl, are both high school students, but in their apartment the kids are still little, and so sometimes they get into scraps and fights over the tiniest thing, and sure, maybe there have been times when they are just jumping around, but even if that's the case, I wonder if they can really hear enough downstairs to justify complaining about it, she says, and her husband replies, that's exactly why I asked you how old she was, you know they say that menopausal women sometimes get hysterical about that sort of thing, but anyway, if you just make sure to apologize next time you see her, say you're sorry for being so noisy or whatever, I'm sure it'll all come out in the wash, he says, as if there were no question that it was her role, as the person at home all day, to do so.

After that, she's standing in front of the enamel sink, washing the dirty breakfast dishes, picking the plates out of the plastic tub of water with blobs of butter and cooking oil floating on the surface, and rinsing them with dish soap, and it's as she's rinsing off the soap under the tap that she finds herself there, a plate held in her hand, staring fixedly at the running water. The rays of morning light pouring in through the window make the rope of water streaming from the tap twinkle and sparkle, and the water sends spray spattering about the sink as it's sucked down into the drain, flowing continuously, ceaselessly, not exactly noisily but creating a slight reverberation as the water and the air echo through the pipes, and the water spills over the rim of the plastic tub, making a faint trickling noise.

It's not a big deal or anything, but do you ever find that happening to you? I guess you don't do the dishes very often, but what if you're brushing your teeth, say, do you not ever just find yourself staring at the water as it rushes down the drain? And it's strangely pleasant, that feeling, of course it's no big deal, but you kind of zone out, as if you're dreaming, although it's not any dream in particular that you're having. And then you come back to yourself with a jolt as you realize that you're wasting water, I guess you just wouldn't understand it as a man, especially one who so rarely does any form of housework, Natsumi said to her husband, and her husband raised his eyebrows in a way that suggested both slight irritation and a modicum of concern, making a face that meant, what are you trying to say, exactly? And of course she was utterly used to that expression of his, but the thing was, she wasn't saying it to convey a sense of dissatisfaction or anything, it was just a minor sensation— the feeling of comfort and hollowness that came from looking at the water flowing from the tap and thinking of nothing, letting oneself fall into a daze—that she was trying to explain, and she couldn't help but feel faintly irritated by the way her husband met that explanation with a suspicious look.

She didn't have any dishes to wash, and neither did she need to fill up the kettle or wash her face or her hands, but she turned on the tap, and there, gushing out from it, was a rope of water, sparkling in the light and twisting like a bundle of strings, or rather a snake, it looked to her like a snake, which made her think about the Japanese word for "tap": you wrote "snake-mouth," written with the two characters for "snake" and "mouth," and she wondered if it was written like that because of the snakelike rope of water that came tumbling from its mouth, but in any case, the water was flowing out of the tap, there was nothing remarkable about it—that was the whole thing, there was nothing remarkable about it whatsoever, it was an utterly ordinary thing—and yet for some unknown reason she kept staring at it, and falling, again for some unknown reason, into a kind of trance.

Chapter Two – The Woman Next Door

AND SPEAKING OF PAUNCHES, her husband had been showing all the signs of developing one for some time now, needless to say he was suffering from a lack of exercise, and though he claimed that he'd played his fair share of tennis back in his student days, she'd never once seen him on the court, and even the Super Gym DX that he'd sent off for from a catalog to try and remedy the situation—yes, even that, you must've used a total of, what, three times? she teases him, to which he replies, I kept it up for three months actually, it was tough, he says, getting genuinely defensive, but of course that doesn't do anything to alter the fact that he isn't lifting a finger, and as a result, it's hardly right for her to go around criticizing other people's husbands' physiques, but nonetheless, it was the time of the year when the weather was just starting to get a bit cooler, most likely the end of September, a Saturday afternoon, and the sight of that middle-aged man jogging as she made her way home from the supermarket was repulsive, really quite sickening, although, that said, if the very same man had been wearing the kind of suit that everyone wears to work, or else dressed in one of those cardigans all strangely similar in both price and design with the appliqué logo on the breast that all those middle-aged guys with white-collar jobs around here wore on their days off, yes, if he'd been wearing one of those with a shirt and loose trousers with no belt, he would have looked like a regular man in middle management that you see all over the place, and she wouldn't have thought a thing of it.

Of average height, was doubtless how he would wish to be described, but from what Natsumi could see he was about five feet four inches tall, and similarly, she figured that while he might have thought of himself as a bit on the heavy side, he definitely wouldn't have wanted to admit to himself that he was obese, or fat, or anything of the sort, and it would've been in getting the results of his company health checkup and being advised to lose some weight that he had finally been forced to admit to himself that maybe he was more than just a little pudgy, in other words, concluded Natsumi, a very well-established type among men of his age.

The flab on his arms and thighs and stomach that was sticking or rather spilling out of his jogging pants and running tank wobbled around like white blancmange freshly removed from its mold, and to make matters worse, he seemed to be on the hairy side, for his arms and legs, where there was of course not a trace of muscle, were coated in hair, and from the places where those slow-moving arms connected to his body sprouted tufts of armpit hair, and all in all he made for such a sight that a woman who lived in the same apartment block as Natsumi, while they'd been chatting on the way home from the supermarket, had said, he's certainly making an effort isn't he, I think he's the husband of Mrs. Okuno on the third floor, I vaguely remember that someone said he works for a commercial TV station or something, but really, though, when you've let yourself become a bleached hippo, a bit of jogging isn't going to save you, is it, and Natsumi thought the expression

"bleached hippo" was so perfect, found in fact the entire re-
mark quite witty, and snickered, and the woman said, oh dear,
did I say too much, and stuck out her tongue and laughed like
a girl, then she said, look, why don't you come over for a cup
of tea? I've been here less than two months, and I don't know
that many people yet, so I could do with the company, and it
seemed to Natsumi that "could do with the company" didn't
mean that this woman was stuck all on her own feeling sad
or hopelessly lonely, but rather that she just had too much
time on her hands and was bored, and she was also very in-
terested to see what other people in the block had done with
their interiors, even if the layout of this woman's apartment
was different from that of her own, so she replied amicably, if
you're sure it's no bother, then I'd love to, and the woman said,
smiling, of course, of course, come on over, and it occurred
to Natsumi that for someone who didn't know many people
and was in need of company, this woman did well to know
where Mrs. Okuno's husband worked, so maybe she was just
a person who craved companionship, and she went up to the
fourth-floor apartment, which the woman warned she hadn't
finished properly unpacking yet and was like a pigsty, and was
served tea and ice cream, and the woman told her that she was
thirty-three and without children, and her husband worked in
computing, and she didn't herself have a job at the moment,
although until recently she'd been attending a class in writing screenplays at the Culture Center (she'd been attending a
fiction course as well, but the teacher droned on about how
important it was in fiction to include all kinds of descriptions
of things, so she felt that screenplays, which didn't need any
of that, where the story developed instead solely through the
dialogue between characters, was better suited to her), and the
story of why she'd moved in to this apartment.

On the horizontally long rectangular plastic and stainless steel plaque affixed to the wall beside the door was printed the room number 404, as well as the water company user number and an NHK subscriber logo that indicated the apartment was receiving a satellite TV signal, and in the transparent plastic section in between, designed to insert a slip of paper, was a postcard-sized piece of paper with two lines printed on a computer in bold horizontal sans serif type

ISAMU ASAKURA
MEGUMI ASAKURA

from which she came to know that this woman living on a different floor of the same apartment block as her was Megumi Asakura, and she also discovered that, of the six types of apartment layouts labeled A through F about which Mrs. Tanabe in the next-door apartment had told her, Mrs. Asakura's apartment was a two-bedroom B-type, the most prevalent of the layout types in the block, and Mrs. Tanabe had explained back then about the area of each of the six types—she didn't refer to the number of bedrooms but rather to their size in square meters—in a tone suggesting that this kind of information would *tell you something*, that B-types as well as one-bedroom A-types were clustered mostly around the third and fourth floors, while layouts D and E were identical in having three bedrooms and a utility room, but that their total area differed because the size of the balcony changed depending on whether it was positioned at the corner of the building, and Natsumi had intuited that Mrs. Tanabe had been trying not even to imply so much as to assert quite plainly that those differences were reflected in the apartment prices, and now, Mrs. Asakura told her, Mrs. Tanabe's apartment, number 605, a three-room F-type with a utility room located on a southeast facing corner, was in fact the *prime property* in the block, and therefore worthy of all of their envy.

Really, though, there are a surprising number of people like that out there, Mrs. Asakura was saying, and with her long, wavy hair tinted slightly brown, and glasses with black Boston-style frames, and gray scoop-necked T-shirt—the kind that clung tightly to the body—and loose-fitting cotton pants in warm beige and a tote bag of thick olive-green canvas from Ichizawa Hanpu in Kyoto, and brown leather sandals with a slight heel that she wore over tights, there was a somewhat mismatched air about her look, yet her two-bedroom apartment was so spick and span, making her pronouncement about its being "like a pigsty" seem almost mean-spirited, and if you were to ask what element specifically made it "like a pigsty," the only feasible explanation would have been that, sitting on top of the dining table in a modern Italian design with thick stainless steel pipe legs (the tabletop a light beige wood, and the accompanying chairs made with brown leather and lightweight pipe legs), were a Ginori 1735 teacup with a fruit pattern, a cut-glass sugar bowl, an ashtray, whose design recalled Mexican folkcraft, with several cigarette butts inside, and a newspaper, and hung on the back of one of the chairs was a cardigan of green cotton lace, and that on the beige leather sofa and coffee table set by the window were a handbag and a few magazines—or perhaps it also extended to the fact that the petals of the colored flowers shaped like white conch shells that bloomed at the tips of the long, green celery-like stems arranged in the tall glass vase of a simple design placed on top of the side table were starting to turn brown and wither at their edges—so that in fact, rather than finding the apartment messy, Natsumi found it much more like a showroom, sparse and with no sense of being lived in, and she said, well we've got two boys, so my place is just a permanent mess, to the extent that you don't know what's what anymore, but isn't it wonderful, though, how a home can look so totally different depending on who's living in it, if you ignore the extra room in ours then the layout of the open-plan kitchen-diner is exactly the same, and in saying that, it struck her that it must be a full ten years now since she'd developed the ability to say things she didn't think at all as if she really meant them, to pass off very standard pleasantries with a serenity that remained unshaken even if the person she was talking to knew she didn't really mean what she was saying, and as she sipped the Earl Grey—as hard as she tried, she still couldn't appreciate the taste of Earl Grey—from her Ginori 1735 teacup and ate the Häagen-Dazs chocolate-chip cookie ice cream that Mrs. Asakura had just bought from the supermarket—she found it overly sweet and cloying, and it left behind an unpleasant taste in her mouth—Mrs. Asakura, who, depending on your point of view, which was really to say, *to a certain kind of man*, might have been considered quite attractive, holding her silver ice-cream spoon whose bowl was square and flattish—at the end of the spoon's handle was a disc with the number 31 in relief against a glitzy peach-colored background, so she figured it must've been a free gift from Baskin-Robbins—in her fingers, swirling it round and round as if playing with it, began, little by little, to tell Natsumi her story.

The apartment she'd been living in before, although slightly smaller than this one, had been very well located in Minami-Aoyama and she'd been very fond of it, but then last year a former boyfriend, whom she had dated for about two years as a student before breaking up after a fight that was really—how to put this—really just because of their mutual lack of experience and a certain youthful impulsiveness, had moved with his wife and children into the same eighteen-apartment block in Aoyama, and the pair had run into each other unexpectedly, and when they discovered what had happened they had of course both tried to play it cool, but now, thinking about the way that neither of them had simply lied to their spouses and casually said that they were old acquaintances or something similar—that's an indication that we were both very conscious of our shared history, don't you think, and what's more, he'd grown up so much since we dated, was so much more settled in himself that he seemed almost a completely different person, she said, and she went into the next-door room and brought back a flat-topped confectionery tin that was beginning to rust around the edges, pulling from the jumble of envelopes and postcards and notebooks and clippings and instruction manuals inside some color photographs, and showing Natsumi a snapshot of a young couple in matching pink and baby-blue polo shirts with their arms around each other, their unoccupied right and left hands (respectively) forming peace signs, apparently taken on the deck of a sightseeing boat on the sea somewhere, saying, this is him, and the next photo showed the two of them side by side in pale-blue bathrobes on the balcony of a seaside hotel, the next was Mrs. Asakura by herself lying on a bed in a bathrobe, and the fourth one was a full-length shot of the two of them on a tennis court in tennis gear—seeing him in shorts made it evident that his legs were short and bowed—which looked like it had been taken with a self-timer, Natsumi thought, and she said, mmm, he looks like a kind person, and you haven't changed a bit, at which Mrs. Asakura said, he was really kind to me back then, her eyes staring off at some point in the distance, and then we picked things up again, started meeting at hotels in Shibuya, and it got to the point that we both realized we were getting in over our heads, and you know, I do love my husband, and I didn't want to ruin the life we'd built together, it seemed to me that if we carried on as we were then we would have destroyed everything, and so in the end, she said, I thought the best thing would be for us to move away, and with that she let out a sigh and said, I'm really sorry, spilling all this on you out of the blue, you must think I'm totally out of my mind, and Natsumi gave an indeterminate smile and said, it just took me by surprise a little, that's all, then cried, oh goodness, is that the time already, I better be getting back to prepare dinner, and when, after they'd eaten their dinner of macaroni gratin and salad with cooked vegetables, she told the story to her husband, and said, I guess those things really happen, don't they, he snorted and said, I read this piece in a weekly magazine by someone who writes erotica for a living. They did a survey of married women living in a housing complex about what sort of affair—or maybe they said "romance"—they would most like to have, and apparently the most common answer by a long shot was that a former boyfriend from their student days would move into their neighborhood, their old flame would be rekindled and they'd start meeting in hotels, that's what it said. Okay, well, then in her case, that actually happened, no? Her wishes came true. Don't be an idiot, surely you can't believe that? Her eyes were welling up with tears as she told me about it! It's totally made up. It's a kind of fantasy, she's telling you about what she wishes had really happened, or else she's funny in the head, it sounds like you're better off not getting involved, and when her husband explained the situation like that Natsumi did start to feel like maybe he was right, but more than that, what really bothered her was the question of why this figure of "the boyfriend from the past" had to appear in this romantic fantasy as it existed inside people's erotic imaginations, it seemed to her incomprehensible, because, even when you took into account the fact that maybe these women didn't know any other men with enough specificity to envision things of that kind, it seemed obvious to her that if an ex-boyfriend actually appeared in an erotic fantasy it was impossible—okay, leaving aside the possibility he'd had plastic surgery or something—that he'd be in better shape now than he had been in the past, and so she had a tough time seeing the appeal of it.

Mrs. Okuno's husband was keeping up his Saturday afternoon jogs in the Equestrian Park, but they didn't seem to be having any effect on his physique, and when the two of them saw him doing his cooldown stretches on the path alongside the flower beds beside the apartment building, panting heavily, Mrs. Asakura would giggle like before and say to Natsumi, you should come over again, but when Natsumi thought about the types of things she might be forced to listen to this time round the prospect seemed like too much hard work, she felt in fact quite wearied by the idea and was in no mood to accept, and had taken to saying, as they reached the elevators, I'll climb the stairs to get a bit of exercise, thereby managing to part ways with her, but she remembered that Mrs. Asakura had told her that she was taking screenwriting classes at the Culture Center, and it occurred to her that maybe the story she'd told her was a screenplay, which, while ostensibly not being very believable— it had, after all, been hackneyed enough that even someone like Natsumi's husband had been able to see straight through it—was nonetheless something she'd either written already or was planning to write, and in speaking to Natsumi about it she was trying to gauge the reaction of a regular housewife to it, and when she mentioned the matter to her friend Setchan—who worked at an architect's firm and had called her up to ask if she wanted to get together with some other friends from high school for the first time in forever (I guess the last time we saw one another was when we went for that meal after Momoko's dad's funeral, which makes it three years ago, although of course Momoko wasn't with us then, so the last time it was all six of us must be much further back, mustn't it?)—Setchan had seemed very certain that this was the case, saying, yes that must be it, although—and here she left a pause—there's this Truffaut film, *The Woman Next Door*, I can't imagine you know it, she said, exhibiting her usual contempt for other people's intelligence, but the plot is almost exactly the same as what that woman in your block described, it's a silly film really, starring Gerard Dépardieu and Fanny Ardant, and Natsumi said, ah, now you mention it, I've a feeling I saw that on TV, I guess it was right after my youngest was born, and I was so exhausted I fell asleep halfway through, they both kill themselves in the end don't they, she said, recalling the plot as she spoke, but Setchan didn't respond to what Natsumi had said at all, saying instead, they were showing it on TV this one time when I was away on business, the woman I was sharing the hotel room with was a very hardworking and capable senior colleague of mine (a married woman), and we were sitting there watching the film on our twin beds drinking whiskey and water, those miniature bottles of Jack Daniel's from the minibar—although when she mixed them it was more like drinking just whiskey on the rocks, she hardly put any water in them at all—and I was so bored by the film, and so exhausted from the trip—we'd had a whole day of meetings with these vile men from the city office—and then there was the effect of the alcohol on top of that, and I must've nodded off, and I woke with a start to find this woman, this colleague of mine, who during the day had been contending so boldly with the city-office men, was sitting there just…I don't know if you'd call that "weeping" or "whimpering" or what, but in any case, stifling her sobs, and I was totally nonplussed, and when the commercials came on she switched off the volume with the remote control and said with a stuffy nose, aah, that hit a bit close to home, her voice thick with emotion, I remember that evening really clearly, although I'd completely forgotten about it until now, I was just so shocked by it, then the next morning she was totally back to her usual self, spouting all this macho stuff to motivate me like, come on, no use dawdling, we've got a big day ahead of us today, and I was just totally thrown for a loot—she ignored Natsumi saying thrown for a *loop*—and there have been times when I've even gone as far as suspecting that maybe it had been a nightmare through which my unconscious was revealing itself—by which I mean that even despite all her macho attitude she is, after all, a woman, and the dream was telling me that I'm actually the same—but probably it wasn't, probably something similar to what happened in that film had actually happened to her, so maybe the story of that long wavy haired woman with glasses is true as well, if you ask me people who have Boston black-framed glasses and long wavy hair are mostly sex maniacs.

Listen, let's say hypothetically that was true of the female architect in your office, but even so, said Natsumi, putting great stress on the "even so," how can you say that the same is true of Mrs. Asakura's story, honestly whenever you talk about romance and stuff you're always so heavy-handed, at which Setchan, laughing through her nose, said, which is exactly why I'm still single, so Natsumi asked, and why do you say that people with long, permed hair and black-framed glasses are all sex maniacs, to which Setchan responded, wearing your hair long and perming it to make it wavy is about emphasizing an artificial form of femininity, more than with straight long hair, but then at the same time, by choosing thick black Boston glasses where the frames are accentuated, thereby bringing out the masculinity and intelligence that spectacles symbolize, you're basically enticing people while simultaneously pushing them away, that's what your look is doing, so what you're trying to express about yourself is: I'm a feminine, erotic entity but I'm an intellectual at the same time, and that's the defining feature of sex maniacs, Setchan said with total conviction in this definition she'd cooked up, you know the trope of the woman who takes off her glasses and transforms instantaneously from a prissy old maid into an unbelievably gorgeous and sensual-looking woman, you find it everywhere, from Hollywood films to shōjo manga to TV ads, she said, reeling off examples, and then the two of them fell silent for a while and Setchan, tired of talking, apparently lit a cigarette because Natsumi heard the gritty click of the lighter, and then Natsumi thought of something and said, I meant to ask, do you know a photographer called Kineo Kuwabara? at which Setchan exhaled through her nose in a way that meant, who do you take me for, so Natsumi hurriedly said, because I hadn't, but last year, my parents invited me to an exhibition of his at the Setagaya Art Museum, they figured it was really close to this apartment and suggested we go together, so we did, and both of my parents grew up in the kinds of working-class commercial areas he photographs—my dad in Nihonbashi and my mom in Ueno—and so they sunk deep into nostalgia, it was a nightmare, but I actually really liked those photographs too, and thinking about it now, I realize that's the last time I've actually eaten dinner out, when I'm not running an errand and not with the kids, pah, how pathetic is that, Natsumi continued, but really what she'd wanted to say wasn't that at all, but rather, thinking about those old neighborhoods of Tokyo and the people who were there, just walking around or standing still, not even realizing they were being photographed, thinking about the moments that the photographs were taken when those people were going about their lives, just as the pictures showed them doing, had given her such a peculiar feeling, filled her with a kind of wooziness, and looking at the photograph of the young kids on the back seat of the bus perhaps on their way home from cram school or something, looking dazed with exhaustion, she had felt so much empathy for them that it had startled her, and when she said this to Setchan, Setchan, who had been listening to her and saying, mm, mm, then mentioned the name of a novelist whom Natsumi had read a couple of things by when she was a student, and said that the novelist had written an interesting essay about that exhibition, so she'd make a copy of it and bring it the next time the two of them met, I think that novelist lives in Mejiro, close to where your parents are, Setchan said, and Natsumi thought that if she admitted to not knowing this then Setchan would think she was stupid, so instead she said, yes, so I've heard.

Chapter Three – Stray Hairs

FOR FATHER'S DAY in June, she gave both her husband's father in Nagano and her own father in Mejiro cotton flannel shirts that she'd ordered from a Lands' End catalog for 5,800 yen each—one in a red, dark-brown, beige, and orange check pattern called "Brick Red" for her own father and the other in a vertical striped pattern called "Steel Blue" featuring bands of differing widths in gray, white, and various shades of indigo for her father-in-law—but what happened, she didn't know if it was because she'd filled in the form incorrectly or whether it was a mistake on the catalog's side, was that the wrong shirts were delivered to the wrong people—her own father received "Steel Blue" and "Brick Red" went to Nagano—and yet as it turned out, both the fathers said that, although at first they thought the design was a little bit bold, and that they'd thought of flannel shirts as being either pajamas or something that young people wore, they'd found that actually the shirts were well made, soft, and comfortable to wear, and ideal for the rainy season when there was still a bit of a lingering chill in the air, and according to her mother-in-law, the shirt had prompted her Nagano father-in-law to start speaking about how, when he was a child and cotton was still hard to come by, he'd had an uncle who'd been posted to some overseas branch of Tokyo Bank, he'd forgotten now if it was Los Angeles or San Francisco, but the uncle had sent them some high-quality pure cotton flannel of 100% American-grown pure Komodo cotton, on one of those rolls like you saw in fabric shops where yards and yards of the stuff were wrapped around a long, thin plank of wood, and that cotton had been very similar to these shirts, with a check pattern in pale red, out of which their mother had made pajamas for the whole family, but he'd said that red was for girls, and had refused to wear them, and his pair had gone to his cousin as a result, and so, he'd said, my siblings and my cousin were all wearing these cozy-looking pajamas, and I was the only one left there wearing my worn-out checked flannelette ones, feeling the cold, and actually come to think of it, our maid Ume was also given some of the fabric from which she'd fashioned an apron and a stomach warmer, and as he was remembering all of these details, her mother-in-law had said, he'd become sentimental, losing himself entirely in his reminiscing, and so, whether it was in fact a mistake on Natsumi's part or a mix-up on the catalog's side, the shirts had ended up being very good presents, and during the phone call she'd made to Natsumi to thank her, her mother-in-law also ended up inviting the two kids over to Nagano for the summer holiday, saying, Shin-chan's in third grade already, he's a proper big boy, and Minoru-chan's in his final year of kindergarten, surely they're old enough by now to come and stay over at their grandma and grandpa's without their mom, aren't they, we don't mind how long they're here, they can stay the whole summer as far as we're concerned, and if they start to get homesick then they can just go back, how does that sound?

When she talked the matter over with her husband, he said, until now my brother's kids have always gone to visit them for the summer holidays, but I guess that this summer, with Kensuke's entrance exams coming up next year, Mizue's decided not to send them, and my mom's thinking she'll get lonely without anyone there, I don't see why we don't let them go, it'd give you a bit of a breather, and it'd do them good to spend the summer in the house that I grew up in, he said, nodding with a satisfied air, as if to say that the place where he'd been raised on the outskirts of a small provincial city was the best possible environment for young boys, and then added, remember when you first came, the summer we got engaged, he got as far as saying, and then corrected himself, saying, no, wait, I should really say, when you first *went*, the summer we got engaged, you were amazed by how great it was there, I remember you commenting on how delicious the air and the water were, and the kids, who'd been to their grandparents' in Nagano a few times at New Year's and in the summer, were very much in favor of the plan, despite its not being close to the sea, which was a small drawback, and they got very excited about it, and tied up in that reaction was the fact that Kensuke, a scrawny little kid in glasses who went around making himself out to be a big smarty-pants, wasn't going to be there, which was excellent news, and also the fact that their grandparents in Nagano were exceptionally doting, and would give the children what they called "rewards" of a hundred yen or five hundred yen for helping out or running errands, so that the kids would start accumulating money as soon as they got there, and they weren't stingy like Mom, and with the strawberries they ate there, which would be cut into perfect bite-sized pieces, they wouldn't be given the usual condensed milk but fresh whipped cream, and during the whipping of the cream, they would be allowed to step in and help finish once it had already been beaten eight-tenths of the way—as it was being whipped the liquid cream would slowly blend with the air and thicken, and there was a terribly exciting and amazing moment when, with just a few strokes of the whip, the contents of the bowl would transform into a mound of bright-white foam, soft, airy, and smooth, but whipping the cream from start to finish made your arms ache, so the kids wanted to help out with just the final section of the task—and not only that, but would be given a hundred yen for their efforts, and when Grandpa took them out driving or fishing, he wouldn't keep saying how tired he was like Dad did, and for all these reasons, the older boy started saying, in a way of speaking that he'd picked up from the older boys at school, yeah man, Mejiro's just way too close for summer holidays, it's not the kind of place you wanna go for the summer, it's super boring, and the younger boy copied that too, saying with excitement, yeahhhhh, it's super boring, and yet Natsumi heard the older boy's voice spilling out from behind the bathroom door, mixed with the lemony smell of the bath salts and the steam, saying sagely, we'll have to get Grandma and Grandpa a present to take with us, a different one from the one that Mom gets them, old people are hard to buy for, we'll have to think about what would be good, and, smiling, she thought to herself that they were actually pretty good kids, her little pair, which gave her a momentary rush of happiness and pride, and even the fact that on her birthday on July 9 they'd said to her that, because they'd been spending so much recently—for Mother's Day they'd put in 1,800 yen and 1,200 yen respectively, according to their incomes, to buy the 3,000-yen potted carnation (*super* expensive!), and in June, for a joint Father's Day and birthday present for their dad, the older boy had spent 620 yen on a handkerchief, including the cost of having it gift wrapped and a ribbon tied around it at the supermarket, while the younger one had given him a portrait of him he'd drawn in kindergarten and a couple of hundred-yen ballpoint pens (in blue and black, that Natsumi had wrapped and put a ribbon on)—and they also had the present for the Nagano grandparents to consider, so, they said, she'd have to make do with this, and had given her a homemade card (with a picture of some roses cut out from a magazine), even that was kind of sweet, and made her feel proud of them, and then before she knew it, the summer holiday had started, the day of their departure was fixed, and their dad bought them tickets for the Shinetsu Line on his way back home from the laboratory.

They decided to send the kids' pajamas, clothes, and books for doing their homework as well as the presents from the whole family and so on beforehand by express shipping, so the two boys would set off by themselves carrying only their rucksacks and stylish stainless steel flasks, and the older boy recorded each stage of their journey in a small notebook, clearly numbering the segments of the trip, detailing how they would get the bus to Shibuya, and travel on the Yamanote Line from Shibuya Station to get to Ueno, and how they'd transfer from there to the Shinetsu Line, writing in also the number of the correct Shinetsu platform, the number of the train, their seat numbers, and the departure time that his dad had looked up for them on the timetable, appending to this his and his brother's names and ages, the names of their school and kindergarten respectively, their home address and telephone number, and the names of their mother and father, saying that he should really write in their blood types as well but he didn't know what they were, and at least, this means that if something happens then people'll know who we are, right, he said with satisfaction, and when Natsumi said, are you sure you don't want me to go with you to the Shinetsu Line platform at Ueno, or if you want we can refund the tickets and all go together in the car on Dad's day off, but at this suggestion, the children both said, as one, no Mom, don't worry about it, we can go by ourselves, although hearing his mother's offer to go with them to Ueno Station or to be taken in the car by their dad came as a relief to the younger one, and he cast a lingering look in her direction, but his older brother pushed out his lips almost indignantly and said, in a defiant tone of voice, of course we'll be okay by ourselves, you can't call yourself a schoolboy in Tokyo if you're scared to go to Ueno Station on your own, and so the younger one's relieved eyes that were trained on his mother now stole a worried glance at his brother, and yet he managed to say in an even more enthusiastic tone than before, he's right, we'll be okay, although he then went over to his mother and shyly pressed himself to her back, draping himself across her shoulders, saying anxiously, we've been before, haven't we, and Mom and Dad were with us so we didn't get lost, but you remember the way to go, don't you, Shin?

Her husband was also leaving for a business trip to Hokkaido that same day, and after the kids had set off, he said, as he always did, right, see you, and was about to go out the door, but then said with a smile, oh, right! you're not going to get lonely all by yourself are you? and Natsumi, who from the previous night had been feeling a dull ache behind her eyes, making her wonder if she might be coming down with a summer cold, said, are you kidding? I'm going to savor the life of a single person, I'm going to let my hair down for once, and in response to this corny declaration her husband said, okay, well I'll call you this evening, and left, and that day she didn't even go out shopping, or do any cleaning or laundry, for lunch she ate the day before's leftover rice that she boiled up with a can of tomato soup like a kind of risotto, dropped in an egg and sprinkled on some cheese, and the final product was so hot that she burned her tongue eating it, and it made her sweat so much that she wanted to change her underwear, and when she went to do so, she found that her body felt very sluggish and heavy, and so she put on her pajamas and dove right into bed.

By the time that she awoke, to the sound of children playing, their shrill voices in the courtyard of the apartment block echoing around that chimney-shaped hollow, it was already past four, and she panicked for a moment, but then quickly remembered that today she had the day to herself, I've managed to catch a cold after all, she thought, and although after sweating and sleeping soundly she felt better than she had in the morning, she still felt reluctant to get out of bed, and besides, once she'd realized that there was no need to get up in a rush because there was nothing that she needed to do for anybody else, she breathed a sigh of relief, she must've sweated again when she was sleeping because her scalp felt moist and itchy, that and the slight dampness of her underwear was less than pleasant, and the door to the closet on the wall opposite the beds was open, so she could see her husband's suits hanging in a row, and the rays of the early-evening sun were shining onto the unmade bed whose cover was still thrown back from when her husband had gotten up from it, picking out several of his hairs on the pillow, which in their blackness stood out in horribly stark contrast, usually as part of the quick tidy she did in the morning she would tear off a length of sticky tape and use it to remove any stray hairs on the sheets and the pillows, and if it was the weekly sheet-changing day—needless to say it wasn't every week, but sometimes she and her husband had gotten into the habit of having sex on the day before sheet-changing day, and back when they were newlyweds, they found that the smooth, cool sensation of the freshly changed sheets while they were still taut and starchy would put them in the mood, and so they'd have sex on sheet-changing day as well—then she'd put all the sheets, hers and her husband's and the two children's, which is to say, four sets of bedsheets in the washing machine in two loads, and of course today wasn't sheet-changing day, but she got up, drank a cup of coffee, changed the sheets, and then decided to take a bath.

While the bath was running, she made the beds, smoothing her husband's pillowcase and tucking in the cover, and with her own bed she folded the top right corner of the cover over so she could dive back in straightaway, and even then the bath still wasn't full, but she poured in some chamomile bath salts that looked like cream-colored rock candy and stepped inside while the water was still running, slowly shampooing her hair and lathering her body. It went without saying that she didn't usually feel as though she could afford to bathe in such a leisurely and luxurious way, her kids would have their bath before dinner, and even on the occasions when she would get in the bath before bed after her husband had already taken his, in other words the occasions when by rights she could've taken her time because she was the last to use it, for some reason she'd gotten into the habit of rushing through her bath and being done with it quickly.

It wasn't like anything in particular had happened to prompt these feelings, but she remembered there'd been times when she'd found the prospect of getting in after her husband totally repugnant, it didn't exactly seem *dirty* to her, she wouldn't go that far, but it was an indisputable fact that when a person was in the bath the sweat that emerged from their body's pores would mingle with the bathwater, and of course she didn't mind that happening when it was her children's sweat, but when she'd thought about the sweat from her husband's body mixed in with the bathwater it had struck her as something distasteful, that was to be avoided if at all possible. She didn't want to immerse her body in water that contained all the dirt that had oozed out of his pores along with his sweat, she didn't feel that way when they were having sex and their bodies were pressed so tightly together that there was sweat running down in the gap between their two sets of skins, but when she imagined the dirt and sweat that had come from her husband's pores mixing with the dirt and sweat that had come from her own pores within the bathwater, she found it revolting, as though the contour lines of her own body had dissolved and were blending, through the boundary with another body and the pores in the skin, with something else—and worse, these contaminations taking place while immersed in dirty warm water—which left her feeling unpleasant, and slightly sick.

She'd spoken to her brother about this at some point, she couldn't now remember exactly when, and he'd said, wow sis, it's a miracle you're still functioning as a couple if you're feeling that way, are you sure everything is okay with you guys, and she'd replied by saying that it really wasn't a major issue, it belonged in the same category of things as stray hairs, the ones that you found on pillows and sheets seemed unclean, dirty like things as soon as they went in the trash, and of course, his hair didn't seem to her in any way unclean when it was growing on his head, but when it'd fallen out and was lying around on top of something, that's dirty isn't it, just the same as fingernails, they're fine when they're attached to fingers, but nail clippings are dirty, right, it's the exact same thing, she'd said and her brother had replied, hmmmm, is it really, though, I can see your point more with hairs and nails and stuff, I guess that stuff is trash, in a way, and I can understand finding them dirty, but bathwater I'm not so sure about, to which she'd said that she read that in Europe and the United States they have a custom that when someone goes up in a space rocket they take along with them a lock of the hair belonging to their sweetheart or husband or wife or child or mother, and when a loved one dies they tie pieces of their hair to their watch chains or weave them into the shape of pansies and frame them, but that hair has been cut off specifically to perform those kinds of sentimental rituals, and in those contexts it seems less dirty and more disgusting in an almost necrophiliac way, Natsumi explained, and her brother said, I guess those types of rituals are tied up with that idea that long hair implies some kind of magical or supernatural power on the part of its owner, right, but whatever the case, I imagine if you told Eiji you found the bath after he'd used it "dirty" he'd be pretty offended, a husband and wife who have sex with one another and everything, I mean, you've got two kids together.

And once he'd said that, it became even harder to admit to the fact that she washed her own laundry in the machine together with her children's, but she didn't put her husband's stuff in with them—because it seemed kind of dirty, she supposed, or in any case, because she didn't want to—and so she presented the anecdote to him as if it had been reported to her by a housewife friend of hers, to which her brother said, well I do my own laundry, so it's hard for me to say but if I really think about it I'm not sure that I'd want to wash my underwear together with my girlfriend's, it feels a bit gross somehow, though I'm not sure why, he said, and after pausing to think about it for a moment, asked her, what about you, and when she confessed that actually she did the same, her brother had said, what did Mom do, I think when you got your period and I started having wet dreams we began to wash our underwear ourselves, but what about Dad's, I have the feeling she washed them separately, at which Natsumi said, you're right, you're right, it's coming back to me, she did wash Dad's things separately, she said, and then felt like that was the normal thing to do—at least in the house she'd been brought up in—and now that she thought about it, from the time she and her husband had gotten married in 1981 until she'd gotten pregnant they had both been working, and before that her husband had been living by himself for almost ten years since starting university, and back in his student days had used a laundromat, but when he'd found a job and moved into his Mejiro apartment there'd been no laundromat nearby so he'd bought a fully automatic washing machine—when they'd gotten married they'd purchased a new three-door fridge with all the latest functions, but decided to keep the same washing machine because he hadn't used it that much and buy a tumble dryer instead with the money they saved—and had therefore been in the habit of washing his clothes as a matter of course, and it wasn't like he brazenly assumed that now that he was married his wife would naturally do his washing, once a week (on the day he had off from work, which alternated between Saturday and Sunday) he would wash his own underwear, socks, pajamas, towels, and casual wear, and Natsumi wasn't particularly amazed that he did so or anything, she just thought that was par for the course, that's just how it was, and she couldn't exactly remember when it was now, she'd already had her first child and quit her easy-but-tedious job that didn't really stimulate her at all (her mother's house was close by, so she could have continued working if she'd asked her mother to look after her son), actually, come to think of it, this all happened in February of the year when their eldest son had turned fifteen months, her husband had caught a bad case of the flu and been in bed for a week, and at the time, they'd lived in a one-bedroom apartment, so it was impossible for him to have a room to himself, and because it would've been awful if the baby caught it, they'd evacuated him to her mom's house while she nursed her husband, although really "nurse" was far too grand a word for what it was she did, which was just simple tasks like warming the plain rice porridge that came in aluminum packs, making him grated apple and carrot with honey, cooling his forehead with ice packs, and because of his fever he was sweating copiously, so she would change his sweaty underwear and pajamas and wash them for him, and it seemed to her now that this had been the turning point, because for whatever reason, from that time on, her husband had begun just leaving his clothes in the laundry basket and so, somehow or other, she'd ended up doing all his laundry.

Up until that point, her husband had been loading his entire week's worth of dirty clothes—apart from his shirts, which he took to the dry cleaner's—into the fully automatic washing machine, and as a result, to call his underwear (tanks, briefs, long-sleeved T-shirts, and long johns of assorted brands such as BVD, Hanes, and Fukusuke) "not well washed" would have been on the generous side, at least in the eyes of someone who understood how to wash things properly, because rather than ever being washed to a crisp white, his underwear was stained by the colored pajamas and T-shirts and sweatsuits he washed in the same cycle so that it looked, to a piece, slightly grubby, and some of his briefs had their elastic ruined by the heat of the tumble dryer, and she got so fed up with his underwear looking like that that one day she threw them all away. In a special offer at the supermarket, they were selling packs of two Fukusuke white cotton old man—or at least "for the slightly elder gentleman"—style briefs and vests for 780 yen, but they were so spectacularly unexciting that she instead bought five vests and five briefs in both gray marl and plain white from

BVD and Hanes, not without some lingering sense that she was wasting her money, and in fact, while she was paying for them at the cash register it occurred to her that soaking the preexisting graying underwear in bleach might've perhaps improved things a bit, and first and foremost, she was starting to have the feeling that the very act of washing another person's underwear was degrading, which ruffled her, but, hypothetically speaking—and *you have to laugh at the very thought* (for some reason this phrase of her mother's popped into her head) because there was no way such a thing was possible—if her husband was presented with the opportunity to have extramarital sex, either as a casual thing or a serious affair—no, she thought, of course I can't come out and say categorically that this type of thing would never happen, but if I had to place a bet, I'd bet that it wouldn't, imagining as she thought all this her husband away on business—then, although it was questionable whether most women would actually think about closely examining the underwear of the men that they were having adulterous sex with, she couldn't really say for sure either way, but this was completely hypothetical anyway, and if this hypothetical woman happened to be looking, Natsumi thought as she stretched out her body leisurely in the bathwater that the chamomile bath salts had dyed to the color of incredibly pale arrowroot tea and that had nobody else's dirt or sweat mixed in with it, only her own, rinsing away the sweat running down her face and neck with water she'd scooped up in both hands, well in that case, then, of course, seeing his dirty underwear the woman would think, this man's wife isn't doing a proper job—and that would naturally apply to everything, not just to the way that she did her laundry, but her approach to all domestic tasks—and then she would start to feel some sympathy toward him for having a slacker for a wife, the kind of woman who in the past would have been called "slovenly," and might begin to think that she wanted to take better care of this man, or else, on the contrary, she would see in that sad, graying underwear something too uncomfortably close to the realities of life and get turned off by the whole thing, but either way, really, it has nothing to do with me (it is, after all, his washing technique of flinging everything in together that's to blame), but for the most part, the kind of woman who causes trouble for married men, going by what I've seen and heard, harbors a malicious prejudice toward "the wife," and so if "the wife" in question happened to be a house-wife, then any such woman would of course assume that the housewife was an entity who would without question wash her husband's underwear, without even a second thought, and so the graying underwear would be deemed nobody's fault but my own, and that idea makes me mad, so it's probably better, in the long run, to have him wear underwear that's properly washed, she thought, and got out of the bath, and, still in her bathrobe, she took the milk out of the fridge, drank a glass from one of the kids' mugs on the drying rack with a yellow line drawing of a dinosaur whose name she couldn't seem to remember however many times she heard it, which she just called a somethingasaurus, and when she sat down on the sofa, the bleak view of the suburban residential landscape—a whole forest of apartments and commercial buildings in mismatched gray and beige that went on and on uninterrupted for as far as the eye could see aside from a few spots of green here and there where trees were growing—which you saw from the window when standing up would disappear, and what lay stretched out beyond the open window was the summer sky, dazzling in its blueness—the kind of sky that seemed like it could suck you right in—and she felt her head growing hazy, despite ly-ing down she began to feel quite dizzy, and it was hard to say whether it was her whole body or just her field of vision, but whichever it was, she began reeling from side to side, so she closed her eyes, and when she looked away from the sky there were orange discs on the back of her eyelids as if they'd been branded there, and on the backrest of the sofa, she saw two or three of her husband's thin, black hairs with a brownish sheen, together with a single gray one, stuck to the raised gray acrylic fabric as if slicing into it, glowing in the light.

Chapter Four – Birdcalls

THE CALLS OF SPARROWS and pigeons she could recognize, and chickens as well, and that of Da-chan, the daruma parakeet that she'd had as a kid, and she felt that the sounds all of those birds made matched up with their appearances.

And yet when it came to Da-chan the red-breasted daruma parakeet who, when he sat huddled up on the perch in his cage, really did look exactly like the round crimson daruma dolls after which his species was named, she didn't know which was his true call. The piercing, high-pitched screech he let out when he spotted a cat on the balcony and grew jittery and afraid didn't sound dissimilar to the kinds of birdcalls that would go echoing through the jungle in nature programs on TV, and it had occurred to her that maybe it was the call of his ancestors who'd actually lived in the jungle many moons ago, but maybe at that time parakeets were in fact impersonating the calls of other birds or animals who lived in the jungle along with them, and for the most part what happened was, with his eyes half-shut as if in a state of ecstasy and his neck with its numerous layers of feathers all puffed up into a ball, he would cock his head and use his beak to deftly break open the shell of a gray sunflower seed he was grasping dexterously with one of his claws, suddenly stop moving, as if he'd just remembered something and was steeped in reminiscences, before eating the shelled seed, making a gruff purring sound, and then, in a strange low voice, both shrill and muffled, saying, *Da-chan, Da-chan, who's a clever boy*, or else he'd imitate the calls of crows or pigeons or sparrows, sometimes the barking of a dog, or even the yowls of the fighting cats that were his enemies, so it was impossible to work out what was real. That was her thought, *it was impossible to work out what was real*, and yet it wasn't as if she particularly cared to know the truth of the matter—in this or in other things—and so, when in spring the bird came and sat on the branch of the bush out front of the apartment block and sang, *tsupee, tsupee*, in a high, shrill voice, she wasn't even especially curious to find out what kind of bird it was.

The younger boy didn't have a particular fondness for animals, but he named the bird who came and sat outside their window in the morning and the evening Tsupee-chan, and would imitate its monotone, repetitive call in his high childish voice, *tsupee, tsupee*, and would go off to kindergarten spreading out his arms as if they were wings and flapping them, and after Natsumi recounted this episode to her mother on the phone, for no particular reason, her mother, who'd never been particularly overzealous about education, as she and her brother knew from their own upbringing, said, out of the blue, it could be proof that he has some kind of musical ability you know, to which Natsumi had laughed incredulously and said, you've got to be kidding, look at the genes in play, even if our side isn't exactly tone-deaf you could hardly say there's much in the way of genetic predisposition, Dad definitely *is* tone-deaf, and I didn't once take music for any of my elective classes in high school, and when it comes to *his* side, I'm sure nobody would argue if every one of them were declared tone-deaf, I don't remember when it was, but one time at his parents' house, my father-in-law was sitting on the back porch overlooking the garden, polishing his shoes, which was a sort of hobby of his, and humming, or singing an eika—that's what you call them, right, those old Buddhist pilgrims' songs?—and looking like he was having a fine time, so I said to him, it's so nice that someone as young as you knows songs from the distant past like that—how old is Eiji's father? I think he said he was three years older than Dad, so maybe about sixty-six—to which he said, oh that song was a big hit when I was younger, I suppose that was all in the distant past, maybe, but still, we all thought Gene Kelly was soooo cool, and when I figured out it had been "Singin' in the Rain" he was singing, I really struggled not to burst out laughing, and my two definitely take after their dad, so when the younger one imitates that bird, it sounds somehow off, even though it's a very simple tune, she said, and yet her mother still maintained that she should allow his budding interest in nature to grow, they sell cassette tapes and CDs with recordings of wild birdcalls, you know that they say that Hikari Ōe developed his musical abilities by listening to those, you should buy him a tape, or one of those picture encyclopedias of birds, her mother kept insisting, you should encourage your children to develop their talents, I'm not saying you have to make a composer of him or anything, just to develop his sensitivity to sound.

The children's Mejiro grandmother had also gone through a phase of believing that the oldest boy had artistic talents, saying of a felt-tip drawing of rabbits he had made at kindergarten or at home—of the three rabbits kept in the kindergarten garden, a white one, a black-and-white spotted one, and a brown one, which had filled the entire sheet of poster paper, with the brown one's ears jutting off the side of the paper, and the one with the panda-like black-and-white spotted fur depicted fat with short ears, so that their grandmother had said in admiration, he's really captured the difference between the rabbit, the black-and-white cat, and the otter so well—that it was so bold and free, really excellent, kindergarten kids are forever drawing pictures of tulips in crayon or pastel, you two were the same when you were kids, and if it's not tulips then it's sunflowers, because their shapes are simple so anyone can draw them, but Natsumi thought, the fact that he drew a few rabbits doesn't mean anything, what's that bunny with the cross for a mouth and two dots for eyes by a Dutch designer called again, Rabbity or something, anyway, he probably just imitated that because it's simple, he's just a very regular child with no particularly pronounced "creative spirit" or whatever, that was what she thought, despite it being her own son they were discussing, but what she said was, that's completely okay, isn't it, drawing tulips, and she bought him a Pelikan palette of twelve watercolor paints and a set of brushes, but in the end he turned out not to have much "creative spirit" after all and didn't use it very often, although he did paint a portrait of his grandmother with an orange head and brown hair, wearing a blue blouse against a lemon-yellow background, and his grandmother, who adored the picture, had it framed at a shop on Mejiro-dōri and hung it in her living room alongside a picture that Natsumi's Yukigaya uncle had drawn when he was a child.

Her uncle, her mother's older brother by three years who had died of a heart attack in 1966—he had spent a long stretch in a psychiatric ward and remained single all his life, and passed all of his time idling around at his parents' house in Yukigaya, and her mother said that he was talented and clever, but he was funny in the head, you had to admit that about him, he really was an odd one, and her father, after saying that she shouldn't

say those things about their children's uncle (the kind of pronouncement on child-rearing that, if he were determined to
make, he should really have made to her mother out of the
children's earshot), said to Natsumi, whose name was made
up of two Chinese characters, one meaning "summer" and the
other meaning "fruit" or "berries" or "nuts," he definitely was a
bit of an eccentric character, but he was the one who gave you
your name, there's something poetic about it, don't you think,
what it means is that, fruit in summer isn't yet completely ripe
but in the fall it ripens, he explained, and from that point on,
in her head Natsumi somehow associated her own name with
the persimmons in the garden that nobody came to pick and
that were eaten by birds, which wasn't a happy connotation at
all, and he then explained that they'd been thinking about Nat-
suko ("summer" and "child") or Natsue ("summer" and "bay")
or Natsuki ("summer" and "life") or Natsumi ("summer" and
"beauty") but her uncle had come along and suggested that
different character for "mi," which means the fruit or nuts that
grow on a tree—he had, when he was at school, drawn a picture of his mother (Natsuki's Yukigaya grandmother), and his
homeroom teacher—who, when he was younger, had nursed
an ambition to become an artist and was to this day an amateur painter—declared it was "like a fauve," and his mother,
who was the subject of this peculiar picture in which she was
depicted with a yellow face and red-and-black eyes, holding a
red fan and dancing in a summer kimono with a gourd pattern,
couldn't see anything good about it, but the young teacher
(who outside of school could be found in a bohemian getup
consisting of a beret and Russian peasant shirt, painting oils
and reading poetry and smoking a pipe, so that he had been
mistaken for a "red") came over to the house and spoke ar-
dently about how they should certainly enter the painting into

the children's category of one of the public art competitions, and when asked what a "fauve" was, he showed them a copy of the journal *Mizue* with a reproduction of Picasso's *Les Demoiselles d'Avignon* inside and explained that the term related to the fauvist movement, and literally meant "wild beast," and the art teacher thought long and hard about what to title the painting, *The Obon Dance* was too run-of-the-mill so they should maybe call it *The Dance*, although perhaps *Dancing Woman* was more fitting for this painting, and after going back and forth for a while he eventually decided that *Dancing Woman* was too artsy and not really suitable for something made by an elementary school child and settled in the end on *The Dance*, and the picture went on to be awarded first prize, Natsumi's uncle was declared a genius, and although it was now over fifty years ago that it'd been painted, the artwork had been well preserved, put in a glass-fronted frame, wrapped in newspaper and stored in a cardboard box, and had stayed like that ever since the spring of 1939 when they'd wrapped it up and packed it during their move from Sakuragi in Ueno to Yukigaya, it was when their Yukigaya grandmother had died and they were clearing out her things that Natsumi's mother came out of the barn, holding the picture her dead brother had painted of her mother and saying, ah, I remember this, look, her voice thick with nostalgia, and meanwhile her father had begun to read from the 1939 newspaper that the picture had been wrapped up in and immediately became engrossed, repeatedly exclaiming in wonderment, I see, I see, so that's how it was, and only then, when he was finished reading, he looked at the picture and said, that's a funny picture—that was all he said, which didn't go down very well with her mother—but over the fauvist-style watercolor painting her Yukigaya uncle had painted when he was an elementary school kid Natsumi preferred the yellowing photograph, slightly smaller than a postcard, which had been packed together with it, unlike the commemorative family photographs stuck in her mom and dad's albums where everybody stood stiffly in their designated spot so you could tell right away that they'd been taken in a studio or someone from the studio had come out to photograph them, this was clearly a snapshot taken by a complete amateur, and her mother marveled, in a voice mingled with tears, I've no memory at all of who took it, I didn't even know it existed—in that small horizontal photograph, on the wooden deck at the back of that Ueno house that no longer existed, a boy of about ten with a shaved head wearing light-colored shorts and a short-sleeved shirt was leaning sideways against the glass window, with just his face directed toward the camera, while close to the stepping stones in the garden, a small girl with a frilly apron and a pudding-bowl haircut was crouching down, hands resting on top of her parted knees, peering at the ground beneath her—it was ants, I was looking at ants, there was a big ants' nest there and I used to leave them little pieces of sugar, although my mother would get annoyed and tell me not to—with her head lowered, and half-hidden by the sliding screen doors covered in woven reeds that separated the deck from the room inside their father was sitting cross-legged, bent over reading a newspaper spread out on the tatami, and inside the house, visible through the window on the opposite side from the one the boy was leaning against, was their mother in a white blouse and gray semiflared skirt, looking down as if between movements. The only person looking at the camera was the little boy, her elementary-school-aged Yukigaya uncle, while the little girl engrossed by the ants and the grandfather whose face Natsumi didn't really remember and the grandmother who was probably younger in this photo than Natsumi was now all seemed totally oblivious to the camera, and on that very ordinary afternoon during the summer holidays, in the garden filled with bright sunlight or the rather dingy interior of the house, they were all facing different directions and doing different things, and when the thought occurred to her that, apart from her mother, who was probably even younger in this photograph than Natsumi's younger son, none of the people in the photo were still alive, it gave her a very peculiar feeling, and when she said, I wonder who actually took this photo, in any case Yukigaya Uncle is looking right at them, her mother replied in a trancelike sort of voice, I have absolutely no idea, and seemed to forget about the photograph almost immediately afterward, deciding to hang the watercolor her brother had painted in her living room, saying that her grandson's painterly touch with the watercolors in the picture he'd painted closely resembled that of her brother's, saying she sensed in it some indication of a special talent, and now she was taking an interest in the younger boy's musicality, saying, do you remember how good your Yukigaya uncle was at the ocarina? You used to ask him to play when you went to visit, and tried to get him to teach you but you couldn't do it at all, and then she said, it wouldn't be impossible for him to have inherited his uncle's musical talents, in a way that made it clear she was holding out high hopes for her grandson.

Sensitivity to sound is important you know, it makes me think about the family who moved into the apartment block the Itōs built who are driving me to distraction, honestly, you can't imagine anyone more insensitive when it comes to noise, I mean I've already had to suffer through all that construction din since last summer, but even putting that aside, I suppose you could argue it's *only fair* that the Itōs got rid of their garden and had those apartments built in its place because of inheritance tax or whatever it was, but still, you'd think they could've been more selective about who they got to move in there. The woman's somewhere between fifty-five and sixty, and then it's either her son and his spouse or else her daughter and her spouse, although going by the fact that I hear her standing there in the middle of the road bad-mouthing the child's mother in that great booming voice of hers, it probably is her son and his wife, honestly, I'm sick of it, her mother said, I really hate this idea of someone living in a residential neighborhood sold off to office workers in the 1950s and '60s having their kids call their grandmothers "Grandmama," and trust me, this particular "Grandmama" is really not the "Grandmama" type, she's so coarse, the sort of person my mother and people from her generation would have called an ex-daruma, in any case she has no class, she doesn't seem to me like a woman who's lived her life as a regular housewife, and when, responding to her mother's tirade, Natsumi said, a daruma? her mother said, I'm not talking about the parakeets, and she explained that in the past "daruma" was a term for a prostitute, and then said, and it's the little girl, the grandchild, who goes out every day on her tricycle, one of those tricycles that makes music when you turn the pedals. You know the "Cuckoo Waltz"? *Cuckoo, cuckoo, la la la-la-la-la la.* Well she goes riding around on it twice a day, morning and evening, without fail. So there's the grandmother speaking with that great booming voice of hers, and the child—naturally, of course—is singing along to the "Cuckoo Waltz." Don't get me wrong, I don't mind the song of the cuckoo, not when you hear it in the morning by a lake in the forest, emerging from the morning mist. Wasn't there a poem that went like that, *the cuckoo serenades the lovers,* or something? I don't remember who wrote it. But anyway, this child who's been brought up with the sound of the "Cuckoo Waltz" blaring out of her tricycle is going to turn out tone-deaf. It's enough to make you sick, I'm in the kitchen in the evening preparing dinner, and I find myself humming along to it too, *cuckoo, cuckoo, la la la-la-la-la la*, and it drives me crazy, her mother said, and then a week or so later, a cassette tape of wild birdcalls and a bird-watching book showed up in the mail from her, and nobody in the house had any particular interest in birds, so they didn't listen to the tape, not even once, and her husband, who'd opened the bird-watching book and was flipping through the pages, said, it says you have to assemble all this gear like binoculars and a rucksack and a cap and go up into the mountains, it sounds like a hassle, and so she replied, there's no need to go so overboard, surely, even if you just went to the walking trail in the forest in the Equestrian Park you could still do a bit of bird-watching, there'd be a few different birds there, for sure, but it wasn't like she had any interest in doing so, and from time to time she'd notice that the same bird was crying out in the same way as it always did, *tsupee, tsupee*, but the younger boy seemed to have gotten bored of impersonating it, and no longer did his own, slightly off-kilter version of the *tsupee, tsupee* song.

She was alone in the apartment in the afternoon one day, lost in thought, when she heard from somewhere far off in the sky a growling noise that sounded like a blend of a car engine and the little roar the gas boiler made when it was lit and the sound of the motor of the washing machine or the vacuum cleaner, and at that moment the lace curtain at the window was caught by the wind and billowed right out, and the clips on the plastic washing hanger on the balcony clashed together repeatedly, and from the tap in the bathroom, which apparently had not been properly turned off (it had, in fact, been a little loose from the time they'd first moved in), there was the sound of water dripping, and she thought to herself that she should get up and try to turn it off properly but couldn't quite be bothered to move, and as she was wondering what to do, her mother called, and the very first thing she said on the phone, without any greeting or preamble, was, did you find out the name of the tsupee bird?—so she gave an indistinct answer to avoid the question, then said, speaking of which, do you remember that daruma parakeet that we used to have, I wonder which was his true call, to which her mother responded, what do you mean by "true call"? so Natsumi explained that what she meant was the call that he was born with, and her mother said, quite flatly, isn't it that squawk-squawk-squeak-squeak sound? isn't that the one he was born with? or maybe that was just his imitation of you two fighting, she said, not meaning this as a joke but really in earnest, so Natsumi said, hah, as if, but she could also see that what her mother said might in fact be true. It wasn't like they hadn't fought, she was four years older than her brother, and until she entered the fifth or sixth year of elementary school and had adopted the mature attitude that she wouldn't deign to engage with children like him, they had in fact had some pretty wild scraps.

It's a good thing that Da-chan's dead, he had such a good memory, if he were around now he'd be singing that "Cuckoo Waltz" all day long and driving me even crazier, her mother said, to which Natsumi replied, yeah, and now her mother said, her voice taking on a note of excitement, but actually the reason I phoned—and with that she hushed her excited voice in an affected manner—is because I want you to come shopping with me. Of course, I'll buy you a little something as well, I have a bit of money, my own savings I mean, not a huge amount or anything, but it's okay to splurge from time to time, do a bit of retail therapy, going to the supermarket every day and only ever buying food and tissues and cleaning products gets so dull after a while, don't you think? The stress mounts up, doing that kind of thing is taxing too, and stress needs to be released from time to time.

It was really exactly as her mother said, and although she wasn't even working part-time, and there were several courses being held as part of the Lifelong Learning Program at the local Cultural Education Center that were relatively inexpensive and didn't sound too dull—swimming (she couldn't swim, for whatever reason); jazz dance; a blade-sharpening course, which promised to teach you to sharpen blades "from cooking knives to hand planes"—and she did sometimes think about going along to a class, for some reason she still hadn't, and when it came to the domestic sphere, where there was no shortage of things to do if she were so inclined, she'd found that for a period of about a year after they moved into the new place that particularly the tasks that fell under the broad umbrella of cleaning or upkeep, all those chores one performed to keep the place in order, were quite enjoyable, more so than putting in the effort to maintain a fully decorated and immaculately preserved interior, and for a while she'd tackled these chores with enthusiasm, but needless to say, that had eventually worn off, and she'd grown more lax with the cleaning, but even then, there was—and she didn't mean to exaggerate, she meant it genuinely—something Sisyphean in the nature of the roster of simple domestic tasks that she had to get through day in, day out, a sense that however much she did there was never any end in sight, and it was only what you might call "family occasions" that brought multifold minor changes to the routine, and the preparations for them, too, I throw myself into avidly and quite enjoy, but then after the fact I get irritated by it all, that was what she'd said to Setchan once, who'd replied that it was the same as with marriages and funerals and other rituals within any particular society, that special occasions were necessary for the preservation of a community, something to punctuate the monotony of everyday living, and it was less that her response was off the mark and more that it sounded exactly like what a stupid person trying to show off how clever they were would think to say, which pissed her off, and so she replied mean-spiritedly, with a liberal splash of sarcasm, what a carefree existence you lead, getting to live your life just as you want to, then, not knowing how to express what it was that she wanted to say, she found herself frustratingly at a loss for words, and then, although looking back now she was very aware how pathetic it was, added, I just think that someone like you who lives alone, doing a job you like, while your parents are living with your brother and his wife, so your situation is much different from Momoko's where you would have to worry about taking care of your mother single-handedly until she dies, there's things that you can't understand when you're in that situation, in other words coming out with the same clichés that housewives always say to single, working women—to "free women"—and once she'd said this she started to believe what she was saying, to think that it really was true and there was of course no way that Setchan would understand what she was feeling, and not only that, but she didn't even understand her own feelings exactly, or how to articulate them, so that when she said, someone as fortunate as you are could never possibly understand, she felt like she'd actually said something real, and had hung up the phone absolutely fuming, she remembered that now, and her mother was saying, if you let stress build and don't release it ... and she found herself saying, wouldn't you say "relieve" stress, in that situation, not "release" it?—when you say "release" it sounds like you're talking about pent-up male sexual desire or something, to which her mother replied, the meaning's the same isn't it, whether it's "release" or "relieve," and so Natsumi hurriedly said, I suppose actually, "release" carries more of a sense of the joy of the feeling suddenly dissipating, but with "relief," the impression is more one of it shrinking away and vanishing, and in any case, she continued in a wheedling voice, her tone rising at the end, if you say that you'll buy something for me then that is, undoubtedly, a feeling of *stress release!*

It began with the New Year holidays, when they would sometimes visit not just her parents in Mejiro but her husband's parents in Nagano, which entailed starting the round of visits before the New Year began, and before that was Christmas, and there were a couple of families to whom they'd send year-end gifts, and December 20 was her younger son's birthday, and if he'd been an adult then she could have gotten away with suggesting they do a joint birthday and Christmas celebration, but since the older boy's birthday was on November 1st and he had his own celebrations for that, there was no way this would be seen as anything other than a dodge, and an unfair one at that, and they would give her parents something for their wedding anniversary in September, and July 9 was Natsumi's birthday, and they'd take family trips during the summer holiday in August and July, then in June there was her husband's birthday on the 22nd, which they celebrated jointly with Father's Day, but she'd still have to give Father's Day presents to her own father and her husband's father, and the same was true of Mother's Day in May, when she'd send presents to her own mother and her husband's, while Natsumi would be given carnations that the kids had bought using the otoshidama money they got at the end of the year, and her husband became housewife for the day, and on their wedding anniversary on May 10 they exchanged presents, and then there was Children's Day on the 5th. In April was her husband's parents' wedding anniversary, and the celebrations marking the children graduating and moving up to the next school year, and on White Day on March 14 her husband would give her a small gift (although in reality, she would buy something and show it to her husband and say, I got this as a present from you), and lastly February was Valentine's Day, meaning that every month of the year contained at least some kind of event, some kind of expenditure, meaning that when she did go out shopping it was always to buy a gift of some kind for one of these family occasions, and there were any number of things that she herself wanted, not the Bulgari rings and Missoni cashmere coats and Ferragamo shoes and all those sorts of things that had in the past been termed "bourgeois style" and that until a little while ago had been known as "high-end brand fashion" and were now apparently known as "luxury designer," in fact these days the idea of walking around with the Etro drawstring or Louis Vuitton Epi bags that she'd bought back when she'd been working in an office and had wanted because they were in fashion (although really, it was less about wanting them and more about feeling like it was essential to have them) seemed to her less crude or uncool than just plain tragic—well, isn't it, though?—and what she wanted was a bag that felt *contemporary* even if it was far cheaper, and she would have preferred a new tumble dryer, and actually a new fridge as well come to think of it, but having said that, both appliances were coming to the end of their life spans, and one day—and in the not too distant future—they would have to replace them, in truth she really wanted a kitchen cabinet with a better design that matched the decor, and there were plenty of other things she wanted, things just for her, but when she thought about "going shopping," what that meant in her head was going to the supermarket near her apartment block to buy food or other essentials, as she did at least every other day, if not practically every day, and by now she was so utterly bored with this type of shopping that she could picture in her mind the way that the goods were laid out before even leaving her house, could visualize how she would go in and, across the aisle from the vegetable section immediately to her left-hand side—containing salad and green vegetables, root vegetables, tomatoes, and cucumbers—were the fruit, the mushrooms, and the dairy products, at the back was a Kinokuniya bookstore and a Pasco bakery, and next to that was the deli counter selling ham, sausages, and Western-style cold cuts, beside that a glass case containing tempura, cutlets, and croquettes, to the right-hand side were the milk and dairy beverages, kitchen products like frying pans, pots, and grilling racks, cloths, garbage bags, aluminum foil, Saran Wrap, and so on, and across the aisle the various kinds of cleaning products, bleaches, and fabric softeners, for the kitchen, bathroom, toilet, laundry, and the rest of the house, cutlery, paper napkins, and paper cups, plastic containers in assorted shapes and sizes for storing food, ladles and corkscrews and can openers and kitchen knives individually packaged with a cardboard back and see-through plastic front and arranged neatly in rows, numerous varieties of instant ramen and cup noodles and cereals in brightly colored packets, and sometimes in the refrigerated display case of the fresh fish section there would be an assortment of expensive fish laid out on top of the stainless steel racks, but it was on Tuesdays that she went there, because that was Fish Special day, which meant the cases were lined with polystyrene trays of tuna or red snapper or yellowtail or octopus sashimi or whatever else was on special that day, and on the shelves alongside it there were always shijimi clams and Japanese littlenecks and Asian hard clams and fresh seaweed in packets, and next to them, in polystyrene trays sealed with film, were tuna chunks and tuna scrape, boiled octopus, rolled omelets, broiled eel, cod roe, squid, surf clam meat, not to mention raw squid, lightly salted cod, Alaska pollock, fresh salmon fillets, rosefish fillets, sardines, horse mackerel, small horse mackerel for deep-frying, smelt for deep-frying, scallops for cooking with, steamed scallops, and scabbard-fish fillets, and in the frozen fish display case alongside were several kinds of black tiger prawns sorted by size, large Japanese tiger prawns, peeled shrimp, shelled Japanese littlenecks, ground whitefish meat, frozen mixed seafood, and scallops, and in the meat section beside it, polystyrene trays containing semiprepared cutlets, yakitori, diced steak on bamboo skewers, meat-stuffed cabbage rolls, hamburger patties, chicken, ground beef, ground pork (with a label reading Guaranteed 80% Lean Meat!), mixed ground meat, and packs containing thin slices and thicker cuts of loin, thigh, and belly meat of imported beef, domestic beef, wagyū beef, black pork, and Specific Pathogen–Free pork, and packs of meat especially for frying in butter and grilling on a hot plate and for making sukiyaki and shabu-shabu, and in the beef display case were the slightly more luxurious cuts of tongue and steak and sliced beef for sukiyaki and joints for roasting, and on the shelves beside that were a huge quantity of ready-made curry roux, various kinds of seasonings, Chinese and ethnic ingredients, ready-made rice porridge in packets, and all kinds of seasonings to mix in when cooking rice, and across the aisle were the soy sauce and other sauces, expensive imported balsamic vinegar and olive oil and wine vinegar, Bovril, anchovy sauce, all the different kinds of miso paste, all the different kinds of salt, all of which she could list from memory just like that, and the other day, on a chilly, rainy day, she'd decided to wear a cotton jacket that was hanging in the closet, which she hadn't taken to the dry cleaner's since last fall because it was barely dirty, and in the pocket she found a single sheet from a memo pad labeled with the name of a bank folded in two, together with a pale-blue linen handkerchief that she'd bought at Barneys in Shinjuku—which she'd thought she must have dropped somewhere—and as far as finding the handkerchief went, she probably had to count that as a piece of good luck, but when she unfolded the sheet of memo paper, she found a shopping list scrawled messily in pencil, and passing her eyes over it, she discovered its contents were the same as the shopping list she'd just written on the MUJI A6 memo pad she used for writing lists, using a pencil taken from the French powdered mustard pot of beige ceramic that was placed on the table alongside the telephone—the only differences being that she had grated cheese and spaghetti left over in the cupboard and so didn't need to buy more, and it wasn't table-wiping cloths she'd written this time but sponges, and toilet paper instead of combustible garbage bags, plus the addition of olive oil—but the fact that, apart from those discrepancies, it was virtually identical made her feel utterly sickened.

Beef mince ~~400g~~ 500g

Can of tomatoes
Tomatoes, eggs, bunch of parsley, milk, powdered cheese, celery,
spaghetti

Table-wiping cloths, toothbrush (Eiji)
Garbage bags (combustible)
Snacks, lunch box snacks

This is what people mean when they say déjà vu, that's what
happens when you become an adult, especially a housewife,
you have this feeling of déjà vu that leaves you nauseous and
dizzy, Natsumi said to Setchan, and because it'd been raining
that day and it was nearly evening by the time she finally made
it out shopping, she was in a bit of a hurry as a result, and had
ended up leaving behind the twelve-roll pack of toilet paper
she'd bought on sale, but only noticed once she'd gotten back
home, so she then had to head back out to the supermarket,
and asked the girl at the cash register nearest the entrance—
she dawdles, that one, she's always the slowest at scanning the
barcodes and operating the register, but she's got a vaguely
pretty face and when she says thank you very much and here
you are, she does it in a childlike, lispy voice, and there's a bunch
of middle-aged men who are enamored with her, it's hilarious,
I've seen it happen a few times, mumbling to themselves as they
join the line for her register, she always takes forever, but here
I am again, oh lord—and said to her, I left behind some toilet
paper I bought, and she cocked her cute little head in a cutesy
little way and said, um, which one was it, and looking toward
the counter with the forgotten items, Natsumi saw four twelve-

packs of toilet paper as well as two different five-packs of tissue boxes in plastic bags, and midway up the stairs just inside the entrance were the three women between middle and old age who had been standing there chatting back when she came in before and were still going at it when she left, chattering away to one another in hushed voices, and in the parking lot outside the bassett hound—the same breed of dog as from the Hush Puppies logo—with its drooping ears and its stupid-looking face that was notorious around these parts for barking nonstop until its owner returned was barking away like crazy, and the old woman who'd been blocking the way by standing in the middle of the staircase to chat with the other women came out singing along to the "Love Theme from The Godfather" that was playing on the supermarket speakers—when I came out they were playing "A Taste of Honey"—and as some children rode their bikes at top speed down the rainy pavement, their mother, who was also on a bicycle, called out from behind them, slow down! slow down! it's dangerous! and a woman of around sixty with straggly hair and a deep frown etched into her face, who had her umbrella open but who you could tell at a glance was not all there, was grumbling away to an invisible conversational partner, and Natsumi hurried through the rain in the same direction as the woman, toward her apartment, and when she got home, her husband, who brushed his teeth far too vigorously no matter how many times she told him not to—she was sure that if it didn't feel to him as if he were really brushing his teeth unless he went at them with such stupid force then that was certainly a sign of gum disease—and owing to that brushing style of his the bristles on his brushes would fray after just ten days so she had to keep replacing them, was playing a game on the console with her children who seemed in that moment like a hybrid between piglet and baby monkey, with all these terrible high-

62

pitched electronic sounds coming from the TV, and sometimes it honestly seems so strange to me, that I'm the one who has to respond to their requests and make spaghetti and meatballs—no, not bolognese, Mom, we want it with meatballs—I mean really, it just seems bizarre, she thought.

The best way for everything to be is placid and uneventful, without incident of any kind, her mother said as she ate her ochazuke with sea bream, at the shrine these days it's always *Family Safety, Success in Business,* and *Good Health* that I pray for, those are the most important things, at some point things will go wrong, I'm sure, I mean leaving aside death, I'm talking about going senile, or becoming a vegetable or whatever, those kinds of things could happen, but up until this point your dad has been pretty robust, he's never had any really serious illnesses, and of course we've had our fair share of ups and downs, but we've overcome them, and here we are, her mother said as she picked away with a dainty nickel-silver fork at a dish of plums and grapes that had been peeled and cut into bite-sized pieces and arranged on top of a small faceted glass plate, then said, honestly places like this are so expensive, it's only with the reduced lunchtime prices that people like you and me can afford to eat here, nodding to herself, and yet it wasn't as if the sea bream ochazuke set she'd ordered was reduced at lunchtime, rather, it cost the same price of 3,000 yen throughout the day, and on top of that her mother had ordered two desserts, the mixed fruit plate and the sweet cooked azuki beans, so her meal had cost 4,000 yen in total, and maybe she'd have understood her mother's point if they'd both ordered the lunchtime kaiseki course menu for 2,800 yen (with one dessert item included), but the evening kaiseki course menus started from 4,500 yen, so what her mother was saying didn't quite add up, Natsumi thought, and yet she felt that if she pointed that out they'd probably get into a tussle about it and so she stopped herself. Then her mother started talking about a letter printed in the correspondence page of the newspaper.

One of the letters sent into the paper, she said, had quoted the famous first line of a novel by—I can't remember if it was Tolstoy or Pushkin, but, in any case, one of the great Russian authors—I'm pretty sure it went something like, and with that she took from her handbag a notebook the size of a hardcover novel, its beige cover scattered with small lilac flowers, and opened it up, saying, I liked it so I made a note of it. After opening the notebook, she began rummaging around in her bag again, apparently looking for her glasses, so Natsumi said, don't you remember, back in the department store, you were making a fuss about how you couldn't read the prices and the labels on things because you'd forgotten your glasses? There are a lot of women like that in the supermarket, aren't there. I've had them come up to me before saying, I'm terribly sorry to bother you, but I've forgotten my glasses, would you mind telling me what this says? And then you tell them, it says 15% acrylic, 85% wool, and the price is 16,800 yen. And the women of that age will say, ohh, it's not pure wool, and then the middle-aged man working in the supermarket will turn around and say, oh but with this percentage of acrylic it's no different from pure wool, and the old woman will categorically disagree, I saw two of them getting into an argument once, the old woman insisting that for something to be deemed pure wool it had to be made of 100% wool, Natsumi was saying, and yet her mother didn't seem to be listening to her at all, holding her notebook at arm's length and attempting to read it, then giving up and saying, oh well, never mind. Shall I try to read it instead? Natsumi offered. No, no, there are things in here I wouldn't want you to see, she said with a smile, closing the book, trying to recall the quote again, tapping her forehead with the tip of her left index finger, oh yes, it was something like, happy families are much the same, but unhappy families are all unhappy in different ways, she said, and Natsumi replied, Mom, that's an unbelievably famous quote that everybody knows, it's as famous as the opening to *Snow Country* or *I Am a Cat* or *The Stranger*, even I know that's the beginning of Tolstoy's *Anna Karenina*, although I've never read it, to which her mother said, hmph, and then, with a triumphant look, so you see? happiness is for everything to be mediocre and uneventful, it's the same in any household—and it's boring. I was a housewife that whole time, and you know how in Letters to the Editor in newspapers and women's magazines and so on, you find these letters from housewives, mostly in their twenties or thirties, who say that they have a lot of respect for other women who have busy careers and also manage to have a husband and kids, sometimes even saying this with some envy, but ultimately for them, they say, happiness consists in being a housewife and making a comfortable home for their husband and children—when I read people writing that stuff, I can't help but feel that it's sour grapes. Or if not sour grapes, then they have to keep telling themselves this to believe it. Because that kind of happiness is monotonous, it's boring. Although what's wrong with being boring, that I don't know. The thing about being boring, having a boring life, is that you should do it while you still can, if you don't have time to be bored, you'll be exhausted.

I'm okay with that, too, Natsumi replied, although she was no stranger to the impression that her life was boring, mediocre, and eventless, a feeling that existed separately from any feeling of dissatisfaction, and today, because her mother had offered to buy it for her—saying, it's okay to treat yourself on occasion—she had not been overcome by the feeling that she had to buy something for her husband and her kids, and had instead bought a slightly high-necked blouse made of thick silk the color of milky tea with pin tucks across the front. She was very fond of it, and her mother had commented, who knew why, that it was elegant and refined and would be perfect for a British-style afternoon tea, although how on earth Natsumi might run into a British-style "afternoon tea" was beyond her, and the slim, stylish shop assistant had said, with the right bottom and accessories, you could wear it to a wedding reception or a concert, which had made Natsumi want to reply, and who do you think I would go to a concert with? but instead she had nodded, and like a well-to-do wife enjoying her shopping trip, had said, yes, yes, I can see that.

Well, yes, I'm really happy with it, but maybe it was a bit overpriced, Natsumi thought, glancing down at the blouse, which had been wrapped in tissue paper and boxed before being put into an embossed paper carrier bag with black cord handles, maybe I'll wear it when I go out to dinner with Setchan and the others, she said, but all the people who were going to be there, Setchan included, were working women—even Momoko, who was single and lived with her mother, was a violin teacher and therefore had some form of income—and she didn't feel very good about the thought of going along to a gathering like that wearing a 48,000 yen blouse bought not with money that she had herself earned but with the interest her mother had accrued when her personal savings had matured from their ten-year term—it was too expensive, and probably very impractical, if she was going to be forking out that kind of money then she should've bought some ankle boots, a bottle of Estée Lauder Fruition, and some wool flannel trousers, which together would have added up to the same amount—and what was more, she'd bought the blouse on a complete whim, but when she thought about whether she had any skirts or pants that would go with it, let alone shoes and bags, and tried to remember all the things that were in the wardrobe and dresser kept in the eight-mat room that her husband used as his "study," she couldn't quite picture any of them going particularly well with the blouse, which would mean that if she wanted to make up a well-coordinated outfit, she'd have to buy something else new to wear with it, and with the mortgage on the apartment and their savings for the kids' school tuition and their life insurance it wasn't like she could just go spending money as she wanted like that, and as she was running through all this in her mind, she said out of the blue to her mother, I've actually been thinking I might get a job, and her mother said, well, if you really want a job then by all means you should consider it, but it'll be hard you know, working outside the house, she said, shaking her head, even though she herself had no experience of such a thing, which doubtless only cemented that notion in her, so Natsumi said, yes I'm sure it will, but you know, everybody's doing it, working in some way or other, and then said, of course at this stage I'm not going to be able to find anything that's remotely impressive or cool.

When she got home late that afternoon, the two kids were midway through a fight, and when she asked about the cause of their disagreement, she couldn't make out what they were saying, although she could fully imagine it was the same kind of trivial thing as usual, still the two of them just kept repeating, but he, he, and, it's because he was, and when she said of the cake that she'd brought back from her shopping trip, in that case I'll hold on to it for the moment, yes? the two of them both said, noooo wayyyyyyy, and the older one said, if it's cake, it must say on the label, please eat as soon as possible because otherwise it'll go bad, Mom, please, he said in a pleading voice, and the younger one chimed in, saying, yeah, yeah, it'll go bad, so she said, okay, but you can't have it until after your dinner, and then asked, what would you like for dinner, and the two of them answered, curry, and, spaghetti, respectively, and the older one said, I had spaghetti bolognese for lunch today, so I'm sickety sick of spaghetti, and prodded his brother's head, at which the younger one said, hey, stop it, and the two of them nearly started fighting again, but Natsumi said, be quiet! I've already decided, we're having cabbage rolls today, not mentioning that she'd already bought meat-filled cabbage rolls in the food section of the department store, and the two of them still weren't old enough to come back at her and say sulkily, if you've already decided then why did you ask, but instead looked happy and said, okay! that's fine! and so Natsumi thought, well, maybe this isn't going so badly, it is, in its own way, uneventful, and like my mother said, there's no way of knowing how long it'll go on for, you don't know how long the *Family Safety* and the *Success in Business* and the *Good Health* will last, and when she thought about the milky-tea-colored silk twill blouse beautifully folded and wrapped in two sheets of rustling ivory paper, in a white box with a Missoni logo, and when she would wear it, and on what kind of occasion, and with what else to match, she felt a sense of dissatisfaction piercing her, and then thinking about how today she'd spent a lot of money entirely on herself, she decided to sculpt the ketchup-flavored butter rice that she was making to accompany the cabbage rolls into star shapes, to please the children. There was of course no way of knowing if in a year's time, putting ketchup-flavored butter rice in star-shaped molds would still make the children's eyes light up, still make them cry out with pleasure.

Chapter Five – Good News

THE FACT THAT what went by the name of a "mixed-tree copse" wasn't actually a naturally occurring group of trees, but rather an artificial copse created to produce leaf humus from deciduous trees like sawtooth and jolcham oaks for use as compost was something that she had learned from the book *Observing the Trees around You* that her husband had bought in a bookshop after moving here, before they visited the Equestrian Park as a family. The walking route through the mixed-tree copse in the park grounds, which was too well preserved to be truly interesting, was actually very similar to Otomeyama Park in Mejiro, although the two differed in size, but the more diverse mix of trees in Otomeyama Park and the greater variation in the contours of the land and the spring-water pond made it more diverting to walk around, her husband said, and her children said, but there are no horses in Mejiro! this park is cooler because it's got horses, to which her husband replied that there were horses in the riding academy in Mejiro's Gakushuin University Equestrian Center, and then smiled wryly, adding, but you can't see them from up close, can you, because the kids, upon seeing the black and the brown horses up close for the first time in the gravel-floored riding arena encircled by fencing had been astounded by their size, and had stood up on the fencing and leaned over in an attempt to see the animals from even closer, but the black horse that had been galloping light-footedly across the gravel suddenly shook its great head and thick neck and bared its teeth—with its top lip curled up toward its nose like that, its face was terrifying but also quite funny looking, wasn't it, the kids said afterward—and whinnied, shook its mane, and thick, tough-looking blood vessels stood out on its neck that was covered in glossy hair, and the sound of the whinnying and the shaking of its neck and its feet kicking the gravel combined to create a thunderous noise altogether fitting for a creature of that size, and the children got scared and sprang down at once from the fence, running over to where their father and mother were, smiling bashfully as they said, phew, that was scary, and an elderly woman standing a little way off with her husband said, oh dear, you're in a bad mood today aren't you, Mr. Horse, what's gotten into you, eh, just as if addressing a dog, and the older child whispered to Natsumi, maybe that lady's brought sugar cubes or carrots or something, do you think we'll get to see her feeding them, and Natsumi was hoping for the same thing, but it didn't come to pass, and after rubbing its neck against the fencing, the black horse ran off to the other side of the grounds.

When he was in kindergarten, her husband had seen, near Mount Asama, a horse giving rides to tourists, led by a man dressed as a packhorse driver, and although that chestnut horse wasn't the sort that anybody would have deemed beautiful, even out of pure flattery, he had been captivated by the creature that stood there as if its sole purpose in life was giving people rides, and had pleaded and pleaded to be allowed to ride it until he finally got his way (the packhorse driver in his momohiki wraparound pants and happi coat said, okay young sir, lifting him up and helping him sit astride the saddle), and the horse's back was so big and girthy that opening his legs wide enough to straddle it was unexpectedly challenging, and he was given the reins to hold, though he couldn't remember now if they were made of leather or rope (of course the packhorse driver also had a rope to guide the horse), and he realized then that he was up in a high, unsafe place very far from the ground, and to make things worse, the horse kept shaking its rump, and I grew terrified that I was going to be thrown off and started to cry, so my dad grew impatient and my mom laughed at me, he told them now, and the younger boy said, in dead seriousness, horses are really scary, they're so big, while the older one said, are you a scaredy-cat, Dad, laughing, to which he replied, I'm telling you about it aren't I, and I'm not trying to hide it, not pretending to be brave is the sign of true courage, which was apparently how he was attempting to teach the children his "life philosophy," and Natsumi couldn't help but think that her husband was, after all, a pretty good type of guy.

Right beside the apartment block, too, was a small mixed-tree copse that looked as though it had been left over from something in the past, and though she knew from the book that it wasn't a surviving piece of nature from when this area of Musashino had been plains stretching out as far as the eye could see and was, in fact, used to create compost for local agriculture, she still considered that the presence of farms in the area—all the fields planted with cabbages and daikon and scallions—signified that the neighborhood was a pastoral one, but this turned out to be wrong, too, and it all came down to farming subsidies, because if you planted, or rather, were seen to be growing even a scattering of vegetables on a plot of "vacant land," it gets treated as farmland, and you're charged a lower tax rate, the super of the building told Natsumi once, and in that mixed-tree copse beside the apartment were a lot of stray cats, there was even a rumor going around that it'd become a dumping ground for unwanted cats, and one of the residents in the block—a woman of about fifty-six or -seven who lived with her unmarried lawyer son—was in the habit of feeding the cats, which only attracted more of them, and they were multiplying, or so people said.

And because there're so many of them, our little Lily (Persian longhair; female; three years old) wants to go and investigate, she's got such a curious nature you know, so she gets right up on the balcony railing and starts meowing and looking like she's about to jump off, it's dangerous, because our apartment's on the second floor, and that's not the only thing, when it's mating season all these terrifying mangy-looking stray cats come to our balcony and start soliciting her, I throw boiling water at them, but it's totally unacceptable, whoever's feeding them should be held accountable, it's a nuisance for everyone, this was what one of the neighbors said to Natsumi, who responded with nods and mmhmms, but the truth was that she liked walking through the copse, she found it quite adorable to see those fat cats of all different colors and patterns come bounding out of the undergrowth, or mother cats go hurtling off, in a great panic, carrying their kittens in their mouths, actually it was fascinating to her to see mother cats behaving in that way, she felt impressed by their maternal ardor, and although she wasn't particularly fond of cats and wouldn't have thought of feeding them herself, they were after all cats and not rabbits, and in all likelihood they weren't going to breed like rabbits, and she felt irritated by the comments that this woman, Lily's owner—who was rumored to have had cosmetic surgery—was making, and was almost ready to reply, why don't you just have your cat spayed then, but it would also, she knew, be more trouble than it was worth to start a new conflict with someone living in the same block as her, it would end up weighing on her spirits, that much she was sure of from the rumors that she'd heard, and so she just gave an indeterminate sort of response, saying, hmm, it's a tough situation, but the Crazy Cat Lady (as the kids in the block all called her) with the lawyer son who had passed his bar exam while still a law student at Tokyo University, would tell her, here I am, making do without a cat of my own, I love them so much but it's clearly stated in the building agreement that we're not allowed to keep pets so I'm coping with it the best I can, feeding the strays is the one thing that lets me feel a bit like I've got cats of my own, all things being equal I'd give them dried bonito and stewed fish bones, but I imagine people would complain about the smell, about the scraps attracting flies, so I stick to dry food, and I've taken a few of them to the vet to be neutered—did you know local authorities will contribute half the cost for the procedure?—and I've found homes for some of the kittens too, found people to take them in, so helping those poor little things to multiply is the last thing that I'm doing, that woman's breaking the rules of the apartment contract by keeping that cat of hers in the first place, you know, so why do I end up bearing the brunt of the criticism, I have no idea how that's fair, I mean in terms of the regulations, it's without doubt me who's, you know, in the right, and to this also, Natsumi would just give an indeterminate sort of an answer, mmhm, yes. Mmm, they're lovely creatures aren't they, cats.

And then, utterly fed up with becoming somehow embroiled in the drama of it all, she found nestling among the mail and the latest copies of the magazines that her husband subscribes to— *Science, Nature, National Geographic*, which, of late, he simply adds to the pile of magazines in the room he calls his "study" without even bothering to open the envelopes—a postcard addressed to her husband with a picture of a winged cupid piercing a pink heart with its arrow, and the words GOOD NEWS!! in big pink letters, and then, at the bottom of the postcard, hammering the point home, the English word HAPPY, also in pink, each of the letters poised at slightly different angles as if dancing:

♥♥♥ MARRIAGE AND ADDRESS
CHANGE ANNOUNCEMENT ♥♥♥

> We are delighted to inform you that Yasuhiko Naka-mura and Saori Watai are now happily married! We've decided not to have a ceremony or reception, so we're writing to notify you of our new address. We hope to see you soon!

Under this printed message was a note, handwritten in teeny rounded handwriting like that of a little girl, "It was so nice to work with you! Thanks for all your help," and when her husband came home, Natsumi said, as she held out the postcard, some good news has arrived for you, and he glanced down at the card and said, what, did I win some competition or something? then, after quickly glancing at it, said, well there you go, Saori-chan went and got married, in a voice that suggested the announcement had greatly touched him, and Natsumi felt a surge of irritation toward both his use of the diminutive "Saori-chan" and his apparent lack of mistrust toward the card's message and overall design, and so she said, don't you think it's so weird to write GOOD NEWS!! for an announcement about yourself? She only got married, that's all it is.

It's a young person's sense of humor, if anything they're at-tempting to make light of it by writing in a more objective-sounding way. Besides, she must have designed this card by herself on a PC, and putting any question of taste aside, it marks a major improvement, when she first turned up at work, she could barely use a computer at all. I like that they're not doing any kind of ceremony or reception, either, it's a fitting choice for a young researcher like her. You do, do you? Well maybe we should've done the same when we got married, huh? This and that are different things. She's still an MA student, and she told me that her boyfriend, this Nakamura guy, quit his job as an editor to become a freelance writer, so they can't be earning much, it seems to me a smart decision. Smart? Yes, it's discreet, and there's something slightly humorous about it. Hmmm, I don't know, this card seems to suggest the marriage of two well-meaning narcissists. There's a pushiness to it, frankly speaking, there are plenty of people in this world who don't think marriage is anything to be celebrated, and to come out and say GOOD NEWS!! like that, I mean, depending on who's receiving this, it might not be glad tidings at all.

Well, it's more welcome than an announcement of someone's death, marriage is good for productivity and all that, her husband said, which made her even more infuriated by the nonsense clichés he was spouting, and yet she couldn't think of a response that would give her the desired effect of having properly deflated him, and while she was thinking, unable to formulate anything, her thoughts drifted to the familiar way he had referred to his colleague as "Saori-chan"—what the hell was that about, and it flashed through her head how when she'd gotten married, in response to her friends and family and acquaintances saying, congratulations, I hope you'll be very happy together, she had nodded and smiled and said thank you, quite naturally and earnestly, with complete ease, but that was just what it was, of course it went without saying that she hadn't gotten married with the intention of being unhappy, but when people said, "I hope you'll be very happy together," she thought of it as meaning something along the lines of "I hope your married life is uneventful and you enjoy it as much as you can," and even if she'd gotten married because her husband actually had some good qualities that she appreciated, like his laid-back nature and the way he didn't get uptight and neurotic about stuff, and that he didn't act all macho and condescending, still she had never felt herself to be unreservedly, defenselessly happy, and needless to say, there'd been no sense of love winning out against all the odds or being consumed by sensual passion or any of that sort of grand romantic stuff, naturally they'd slept together before marriage, and though it hadn't been completely mind-blowing or anything, at least if she compared it to the sex she'd had with other men (although in fact, she'd only had sex with two people other than her husband), she felt like he'd understood that her sensuality was a holistic, whole-body kind, and on top of that, they did just get along quite well, which seemed to be proven by the fact that when she'd told him about how she'd written in an elementary school writing exercise that when she grew up she either wanted to own a bird shop or be like her Yukigaya uncle he'd found it funny, and because of that, he'd said to her, I can't draw as well as your Yukigaya uncle, I can't play the ocarina either, I'm not a weirdo, and I won't be able to just hang around and play with you all the time, but will you marry me anyway— that had been his marriage proposal, he hadn't added anything else to it, such as, I think I can make you happy regardless, or any of the other things that he should have appended to it, and yet despite this proposal of his, he had the gall not to find anything embarrassing about this marriage notification, she didn't like this unconscious show of ignorance that he was putting on, and at any rate, they hadn't sent out that kind of wedding notification themselves, they'd leafed through a book of samples in a small printing shop on Mejiro-dōri and had chosen a very safe, standard message beginning with the appropriate seasonal greeting and the shop printed it for them, to begin with it wasn't clear if their marriage—which would next year enter its tenth year—was all that happy or *good*, of course she didn't actively think it was *bad*, but at least, when they'd been preparing the announcement postcard, she hadn't been happy enough to spell it out in dancing letters from the Roman alphabet like that, we were a lot more low-key, she said, and she remembered that in a small color booklet entitled *Handy Information Booklet* that the newspaper delivery boy who'd come in the morning to collect her money had given her, along with the paper bags for putting the old papers in to be recycled, saying, as he always put it, these are for you if you'd like them, was an article called "Etiquette for Celebrations and Condolences," which contained a chart of Wedding Anniversary Presents, and she went to take the *Handy Information Booklet* out of the black magazine rack, a modernist Italian design in hard plastic that was on permanent display at MoMA and that her husband's friends had bought for their wedding anniversary—it hadn't really gone with the rooms of the two apartments they'd lived in until now so they hadn't used it, but in this current apartment it matched both the feel of the room as a whole and the dining table that they'd gotten hugely discounted in a sale, and so they were finally putting it to use—and read from it out loud, saying, *A wedding anniversary is the time when we commemorate the founding of a family. There are lots of ways of making wedding anniversaries into special family occasions each and every year, including the exchange of gifts, going out to eat at a special restaurant, taking a little minibreak just the two of you,* and then she said, reading this it really struck me that a marriage is a thing that won't last unless you put in the effort of maintaining it, you have to create a special commemorative day and actively remember the fact that you got married.

First anniversary: paper, suitable gifts: paper items (notebooks, photograph albums, etc.); second anniversary: cotton, suitable gifts: cotton items (handkerchiefs, scarves, etc.); third anniversary: leather, suitable gifts: leather items (bags, wallets, boots, etc.); fourth anniversary: book, suitable gifts: books; fifth anniversary: wood, suitable gifts: wood items (saplings, chopsticks, decorative objects, etc.); sixth anniversary: iron, suitable gifts: iron items (pots and pans, etc.); seventh anniversary: copper, suitable gifts: copper items (vases, mugs, etc.); eighth anniversary: bronze, suitable gifts: electrical appliances; ninth anniversary: pottery, suitable gifts: pottery items (plates, coffee cups, etc.); tenth anniversary: tin, suitable gifts: tin items (pans, kettles, spoons, etc.); eleventh anniversary: steel, suitable gifts: kitchen items; twelfth anniversary: silk, suitable gifts: silk items (blouses, scarves, etc.); thirteenth anniversary: lace, suitable gifts: lace items (handkerchiefs, tablecloths, etc.); fourteenth anniversary: ivory, suitable gifts: personal seals, chopsticks, etc. (NB: Owing to the global ban on the trade of ivory products brought in to conserve the African elephant, this might be difficult); fifteenth anniversary: crystal, suitable gifts: jewelry, watches, ornaments, this is where it stops going through them year by year, from now on it's every five years, *twentieth anniversary: china, suitable gifts: china items (tea utensils, teacups, coffee cups, etc.); twenty-fifth anniversary: silver, suitable gifts: silver items (accessories, silverware, etc.); thirtieth anniversary: pearl, suitable gifts: pearl accessories; thirty-fifth anniversary: coral, suitable gifts: accessories, ornaments; fortieth anniversary: ruby, suitable gifts: ruby accessories or ornaments; forty-fifth anniversary: sapphire, suitable gifts: sapphire accessories or ornaments; fiftieth anniversary: gold, suitable gifts: gold items (accessories, goblets, etc.); fifty-fifth anniversary: emerald, suitable gifts: emerald accessories or ornaments;*

sixtieth/seventy-fifth anniversary: diamond, suitable gifts: diamond accessories or ornaments, and so it goes on, what I'm trying to say is, why do people need to do all of this to commemorate their wedding and reassure themselves that they're married, that's what I want to know. And now we have to give that "happy" bride a gift to celebrate her marriage, right? In this article, it says that, according to a study by the Home Consultancy Department of Sanwa Bank, you should give whatever it would have cost to attend the wedding, for a colleague the going rate is 20,000 yen, isn't it, although I guess you can halve that if there's no party, but at any rate, that'll come out of your allowance, yes? Natsumi said and then, after a little pause, continued, as she opened her beer, but honestly, don't you think this kind of wedding announcement is too *excitable*? You don't think it's dumb? To be frank, I think it's pathetic, and dumb.

It's okay to be a bit excitable, isn't it, that way people will know how pleased they are to be married, her husband said, adopting a conciliatory attitude that meant he was attempting to avert an argument and smooth over the situation, and Natsumi poured some beer into her glass and drained it all at once and then said, in an irritable tone of voice, of course the whole thing of doing away with the reception and party and just informing us of their new address is a good thing, if that was the whole story then I'd even go so far as to say it seemed somewhat intelligent, but what are they going to do when they have to alert people of their divorce, are we going to get a postcard saying SAD NEWS!! and there'll be a picture of a blue heart ripped in two, and when their parents die it'll be TERRIBLE NEWS!! with a picture of crying angels, is that what they're going to do? to which her husband said, wait, are you drunk already, which was clearly his way of trying to tell her in a humorous way that he was fed up with discussing it, and

Natsumi said, so damn stupid, and got up from her chair and went into the small six-mat room, slamming shut the sliding door between that room and the living room, and as she was muttering to herself, just the sight of you makes me sick, she heard her younger boy who'd just gotten out of the bath, saying, hey, where's Mom? There's no pajamas laid out for us! No pajamas, no pajamas! all that in a high-pitched, cutesy voice, clearly in a good mood, and she heard her husband saying, okay, okay, Dad'll put your pajamas on for you tonight, they're in the drawers in your room, aren't they? and she heard him getting up from his chair.

Chapter Six – The Cat Debacle

THE OLDER BOY, who took after his father and was a little chubby, fell from an iron bar in the playground—he'd also inherited his father's lack of coordination, as well as the strangely obstinate streak in his nature, or so Natsumi would think whenever he got on her nerves—and although thankfully he hadn't broken anything, he'd fallen backward headfirst and reached his hands out to the ground to protect his head, and while his arms were chunky the bones were actually quite thin, and under the ample weight of his body his wrist had twisted at a funny angle and he'd sprained it, it'd swollen up to a ludicrous size, so he'd needed to go to the surgical and orthopedic hospital nearby, and in the waiting room there, the boy had reported to her as soon as he came home, his eyes as round as saucers, Mom, Mom, you know that woman who lives in this block, you know the really flashy woman with the huge white cat, I could tell it was her by her voice, but really, at first I thought she was a ghost, it was unbelievable, half her face was all swollen up and purple, it was like some kind of special effect from a film or something!

At least, that was what he said, I wonder what happened to her, she said to her husband, to which he replied, maybe she got stung by a poisonous insect or something, or touched some poison ivy and got a rash, and when the older boy had started to describe to his brother in great detail the SFX-style wounds on the woman's face Natsumi had told him off, saying, you stop that right now, the poor woman is sick, you should feel sorry for her, but now, when she said to her husband, it must be *maddening* for a *gorgeous woman* like that to have half her face swollen up all purple, she placed a lot of emphasis on the words "maddening" and "gorgeous woman," and although her husband wasn't the particularly observant type, he did notice the accentuation, and smiled wryly, saying, is she really that *gorgeous?* to which Natsumi said with great enthusiasm, oh my goodness, you have no idea. People say she must've had some work done on her eyes and her nose, I swear they're the exact same eyes and nose as Mieko Hirota and What's-Her-Name Kokonoe, it's a really dated style of plastic surgery, not in fashion now at all. Are there fashions when it comes to faces? Of course there are, you can't change them over all that quickly but there are definitely trends, and also, according to Mrs. Hirano from the seventh floor (you know the woman whose husband is an editor of a weekly magazine), the gorgeous woman—I've heard that her husband is a securities trader—used to work at a club in Ginza, Mrs. Hirano went there a lot when she was dating a novelist, and she said she was so surprised to run into that same woman right outside our apartment block, saying, she's a nasty, stuck-up piece of work. Even on hearing that, though, her husband simply made a disinterested mmm noise, and started to read the sports section of the paper, and so although she hadn't really expected a huge reaction from him, she said, you could at least show a little interest when I'm gossiping about the neighbors.

The following day, by the trash and recycling area beside the parking lot, she ran into the woman that the kids called the Crazy Cat Lady together with Mrs. Hirano and the super, all standing there with grim expressions on their faces and their arms folded, nodding seriously, so she said, what's happened? to which Mrs. Hirano said, well, lowering her eyebrows into a frown, then said to Mrs. Nakamura a.k.a. Crazy Cat Lady, you said it was ten days ago, Mrs. Nakamura nodded gravely, and Mrs. Hirano went on, they found a dead cat, in the copse over there, but the thing is, it doesn't seem to have died naturally, oh! it's so horrid, at which Mrs. Nakamura took over, saying in a trembling voice, it must've been that woman who did it, and the short, feeble-looking super in his gray uniform looked somewhat troubled, and said, well, we still don't know for sure who's responsible, I've heard talk of middle schoolers in this neighborhood who go around attacking homeless people and calling it "hobo hunting," so it could well be them up to their tricks again, he trailed off, and Mrs. Hirano, looking sharply at the super, said, but weren't you saying that one of the residents was asking you to call the local animal control to see if someone could come to exterminate or vacate the stray cats around here, and you told me that you'd said to them that the public health center would take away stray dogs but they didn't do that for stray cats, and Mrs. Nakamura, who already had tears in her eyes, said, it had been doused in boiling water, all the fur on its back and half of that on its head had peeled off, and one of its eyes had popped out like a quail's egg, it was such a good-natured stray as well, that one, a tabby with a long tail, with lovely green eyes, she said, beginning to choke up, and Mrs. Hirano, letting out a sigh, said, again, oh, it's just so awful, she always used to say, didn't she, that when strays came to her balcony to try and tempt her own cat away that she'd fling boiling water at them? it's true isn't it? she said to Natsumi, and Natsumi said, yes, well, and then, without thinking, or maybe more semiconsciously, she passed on the information that her son had seen the woman at the hospital yesterday, at which Mrs. Hirano said, well! and opened her eyes very wide, and the super let out a guttural hmmm noise and Mrs. Nakamura's eyes shone in a way that you could feasibly have described as "glinting," and Mrs. Hirano said, come to think of it, I've barely seen her at all lately, and when I passed her yesterday she was wearing a gray cap with a thin brim like this—she moved both her hands to describe the shape of the hat—made from the same fabric you'd use for suits, and a black veil, and I remarked admiringly to myself on her retro taste in fashion, but there you go, now it all makes sense, how awful, for that to happen to your face, she said and then, after a pause, lowering her voice, continued, you know what.

It must be the Curse of the Cat.

Hmmm, the super said, ambiguously, feebly.

That's right, Mrs. Nakamura said, with total conviction.

There's no doubt about it, even if, hypothetically speaking, her face got that way because of the surgery (you know they inject formaldehyde and silicone and all kinds of things in there? aren't you thinking about breast enhancement? hers is on the face), the cat's resentment will still be involved somewhere down the line, it must be, don't you think, Mrs. Nakamura, Mrs. Hirano opined, and Mrs. Nakamura nodded with a fixed expression, and the super said, uncomfortably, well, in any case, let's just keep that between ourselves, okay, other people have been complaining about the stray cat issue too, and it wouldn't be good for nasty rumors to spread, it'd be a real problem if that kind of talk got out, let's just keep it between us, he said, although clearly, he knew full well that that was not how things were going to go.

Can you imagine, it was a nightmare of a conversation, Natsumi reported that evening to her husband after the children had gone to sleep. Leaving aside the curse, though, I really do think it was her that poured boiling water on the cat, there's something wicked looking about that woman's face, you know she boils water in a saucepan and then takes it out to the balcony to fling at the cats, there's something definitely not right about her! I'm not going to speak to her anymore, she said in a tearful voice, and though her husband said, you should try not to get too involved, he did also say, that's a vile thing to do, and for once sounded quite indignant, and then, in total seriousness, added, I don't think it's true about the curse of the cat, this isn't some elementary school urban legend, and then added, although, I can also see that they might actually turn out to be right.

There's a reason I say that, her husband began, as he mixed himself a weak whisky and water. Which is that I remembered a story that my grandma told me, she was the daughter of a middle school English teacher and had gone to a prefectural girls' school (it had a swimming pool even back in those days, which just goes to show you how seriously the people in Nagano take children's education), and she was, I suppose, what you'd call a member of the intelligentsia insofar as it existed in the countryside at that time, but her faith in the curse of the cat was unwavering, it went back to when she was in elementary school, which must have been, oh, around about 1910 or 1915 or so, and near her house was a fishmonger's run by a couple from Kashiwazaki in Niigata, and she used to always say that the fishmonger's had the curse of the cat on it, I'd forgotten all about this story, but it suddenly came back to me, I don't know if it really was a curse or not, but anyway, it scared me, her husband said, laughing.

When I was a boy it was a very regular sort of fishmonger's with a refrigerated glass showcase, and the girl from the fishmonger's was in the same year at school as me—she was a lovely little girl with pale skin and a slender, oval face, the kind that you imagine when you think of the classic Niigata beauty, and she was always top of the class, and I was second—and so I only half believed what my grandma said, or more like I thirty-percent believed it, but according to her, it had been a dark, grimy shop with wooden boxes full of fish spread out across the dirt floor, and her father, who was an English teacher, had forbidden her mother from buying fish from there because it wasn't clean, but the woman who worked there was a real rough old hag with a ferocity of spirit to rival any man's, and she had an antipathy to the thief-cats in the neighborhood that would come to steal the shop's fish, and of course, as a fishmonger what they could have done is, instead of throwing away all the scraps from the fish that they couldn't even sell as trimmings, they could've given them to the cats and then they wouldn't have had the problem in the first place, but as it was, as soon as this woman spotted a cat she'd go crazy, and would chase it away and throw water at it, and so it only stood to reason the cats would target the fish—I wasn't quite sure why this meant it "only stood to reason," but that was what my grandma would say with great seriousness, her husband explained—and one day a big thief-cat that was attempting to escape from the shop with a splendid sea bream in its jaws—and at this point her husband recalled how the old-fashioned word "thief-cat" always appears, not just in period films and novels but also on TV, as an insult used by

86

the wife to describe their husband's lover, and said, I wonder if wives actually used that word in real life about their husbands' lovers, and Natsumi, feeling somewhat irritated by the digression the story was taking, answered, I'm guessing people who really hate cats use an idiom like that, to which her husband nodded, saying, yeah, I guess so, actually, now that I think of it, I just remembered something I read in the correspondence page of the newspaper, I think it must have been a special feature on educating children or something, because there was this letter I read by a housewife in her late forties, which explained that as a child, when she'd completed some minor chore her father had asked of her, like going to the kitchen to change his ashtray or fetching the newspaper from the newspaper box, he would pat her head and say, *nekomashi, nekomashi*, and so she'd always thought that it was a term of praise, and had felt a burst of pride whenever he'd said it, until one day she'd found out that the word actually meant that she was *better at least than a cat*, and had been terribly upset by this and had hated her father for it, and the point of her letter was that adults' careless word choices can wound children's pure hearts, so maybe that's another case of someone who detests cats, probably if this was America they'd call it "emotional abuse of children" or something like that, he said, for once really quite loquacious, and reading this reminded me that when I was in kindergarten, my dad would give me two or three chores to do at the same time, I'd be told to go and get the newspaper from the newspaper box and, *while I was there*, to get an ashtray and matches from my mom in the kitchen, and so on, and of course I'd forget things, right, I'd forget the matches or whatever. And after he'd pointed out what it was that I'd forgotten, my dad would say, well, I guess at least you're better than a cat, in other words, he'd essentially use this phrase to imply that I wasn't careful enough, so I'd be embarrassed when he'd say it, but because I never suspected that I was being praised, I didn't ever feel hurt, and this idea of saying someone is better than a cat is ultimately just a silly gag, even if it's a slightly sarcastic one, and in the case of the woman who wrote the letter, her father was probably just bad with words, and he'd actually intended to be praising her, it's a funny old story, to which Natsumi said, I know the expression *I'd gladly accept help even from a cat*, but that's the first time I've heard *nekomashi* or *better at least than a cat*, but anyway, leaving that aside, what happened with the woman from the fishmonger's, you were talking about the curse of the cat, she said, attempting to get the narrative back on course, but then added, I'm glad that it exists, though, it's a good phrase, *nekomashi*.

Watching the cat attempt to run off with a magnificent sea bream in its jaws, the woman from Uomasa Fishmonger hurled one of her fish knives at the cat, it goes without saying the knife was well sharpened and had a fine blade, and it lopped one of the cat's hind legs clean off, or so my grandmother said, although thinking about it now, even if it was sheer coincidence that the knife didn't land in the cat's stomach then it was a very lucky coincidence (that cat lived for several more years with three legs, apparently), and not long after that, the woman from the fishmonger's fell from the second-floor window—the wooden railing on the window had rotted and grown weak—and broke her leg, and although she should have gone to a proper hospital she didn't want to spend the money, so went instead to a bonesetter, who was also a judo instructor and didn't have a very good reputation, but the leg never healed properly and she walked with a limp for the rest of her life, people used to say that it was the curse of the cat, and after the war, her grandson grew incensed because there was a particular cat that kept going after his pretty white racing pigeons, which he kept in a drying rack that he'd converted into a pigeon loft, and had one day tried to scare the cat away by firing his air gun, but by sheer coincidence, one of the bullets had struck the cat and killed it, the cat had killed two or three of the grandson's pigeons in the past but its owner had compensated him, and above all, it was hardly right to go shooting an air gun around the town, the people in the neighborhood said in outrage, but the grandson, who was a meth addict, had been a delinquent since middle school and there were rumors that he hung around with the yakuza, or else that he was in fact a full-fledged member, and so people were frightened that if they kicked up a fuss about it publicly then it wouldn't be a cat that got shot next time but them, so they avoided confronting him, but in the end he was shot with a rifle in a yakuza clash and died—there was a long article in the local newspaper with photos and everything—and that was, needless to say, the curse of the cat, as was proven by the fact that the place that he was shot and the place that the cat was shot were one and the same, and so my grandma used to say that the people from the fishmonger's family all had the curse of the cat on them, her husband said, and Natsumi exhaled, saying, wow, I see.

She had a strange feeling when it came to the curse of the cat, as if she both understood it and didn't at the same time, clearly her husband didn't seem to be telling lies or horror stories, and this was something he'd heard as a child from his grandmother, but it was the first time that she'd heard him speak of it, and so she asked, but did you believe it? did you believe in the curse, when you were a kid? and by the point that he came out and said, of course I never bothered to check the facts, and thinking about it now, I'm not sure if it ever occurred to me to ask my dad whether or not it was true, but you know what, I just thought of something, it's thanks to that very story that I married you, he was coming to the end of his third glass of the twelve-year-old Ballantine's—the drinks he mixed got stronger each time—that her parents in Mejiro had received as a midsummer gift, but had passed on to him since her father didn't drink whisky and so she said, now you're just spouting drunken nonsense, and laughed, but he said, I can't deny that I'm drunk, but that doesn't take away from the fact that I've just realized that it's the truth, he said, we first met, in an extremely ordinary way, as friends of the bride and groom, respectively, at a wedding party at a Mexican restaurant (I've forgotten its name now), and not only did we get in a taxi together because our homes were in the same direction—of course, that played a big part in bringing us together too—but a little while before, I'd found a kitten crouching in the bushes outside the entrance to my building, shaking like a leaf, it wasn't doing very well, so I brought it up to my apartment, I couldn't tell what was wrong with it but I could see it was sick, and I took it along to a nearby vet, where they told me that one of its front legs was broken and it was generally quite weak so it was best if they kept it at the vet for two or three days, and it was during that time that we rode the taxi together, and when I told you about it, about how I'd gone and picked up this cat, but my apartment contract stated I wasn't allowed to have pets, and I lived alone and wasn't at home much, and I didn't know what I was going to do with the kitten once its leg was better, you responded without any hesitation, in a very no-nonsense way, in that case I'll take it in, my mother has too much spare time on her hands and loves having something to take care of, so they'll keep each other company, and I was so struck by what a generous person you were, after that we started going out, and I'm pretty sure this was all because of the principle I'd internalized from my grandmother that you have to be kind to cats, and if it wasn't for that kitten, I really have no idea what we would have talked about in that taxi back from Shibuya—hmm, that's true, if I'm introduced to friends of the groom at weddings and start asking them a bunch of questions they get nervous that I'm trying to assess their worth as a potential husband or something, there are women who size up men in such a transparent way, aren't there—which means that it's pretty much that cat that brought us together, he said, and Natsumi couldn't deny that, yes, everything he was saying was true, although for her part, needless to say, she hadn't had the slightest sense at the time that she'd just found the person she was going to marry, she'd just thought of her mother and how, whenever there was an ad on TV with a cat in it, she would say to Natsumi—or rather, it was more like she was saying it aloud to herself, not really expecting a reply—oohhh, loook, loook, it's so cute, maybe I'll get a cat, you know they say everyone's getting one these days, and she'd said, without really thinking too much, in that case, I'll take it and give it to my mother as a present, she's got plenty of spare time and mentioned she wanted one, and the man in the seat next to her—the one behind the passenger seat—had let out a kind of yelp, a combination of surprise and joy, and said, what, are you serious, oh that's such a relief, I'm sure cats are much happier when they're kept in proper homes, sounding genuinely touched, and in the afternoon two days later, which was a Sunday, he'd come around with a book about cat ownership and a packet of dry cat food along with the kitten, which he'd placed on a towel laid out in a shoebox that had once contained Hush Puppies walking shoes—with the picture of the trademark, bovine-looking puppy with those floppy ears on it—which he held gently in both hands, and after he'd had a cup of tea and a slice of cake and had gone home, her mother, who'd set the quiet, frightened kitten with the black-and-white mottled fur that still had a cast on its leg at her knee, and was stroking it,

said to Natsumi, so? and Natsumi, who had immediately understood the meaning of this extremely concise question, ignored
it with a grunt, at which her mother said in an impatient tone,
he's kind, and he seems like a good person, out of everybody
you've brought back here so far I think he's the best, she said,
getting way ahead of herself, and then added, I asked him back
next Saturday, to check up on the cat and have dinner, she said
wrinkling her nose and smiling in a self-satisfied way.

The kitten, which they ended up calling Bandy after the
bandage on its leg, was very weak, as often happens with cats
that have been born stray, and after its leg had healed it got
rhinitis and diarrhea that wouldn't go away, in the end it died
within six months, but during those six months Natsumi and
her husband got engaged, and her mother cried as she said, it
was Bandy who brought you two together but he never got to
see you in your wedding dress. She said that she didn't need an
engagement ring on which, according to surveys carried out by
banks and etiquette books about celebrations and commisera-
tions, it was standard for the man to spend the equivalent of between three and six months' salary, but they decided that they
would have a regular sort of ceremony, and although really
she wanted to give up her job (an admin role at a hairdressing
college, which she'd gotten through her parents' connections)
because she found it a pain, she decided nonetheless to keep on
working until she got pregnant.

About a month after that, when Natsumi ran into Mrs. Hirano
and Mrs. Nakamura, they told her that although nobody knew
any details about what had happened to the facial swelling,
Mrs. and Mr. Murakami had moved into a riverside high-rise
apartment block, and then they said, in a whisper, that the way
they'd moved had been so hasty, so quick, that they must've

been scared of *you know what,* and Natsumi wondered if the two women might have been feeling slightly remorseful about the way they'd been spreading exaggerated reports of the incident to the other residents, thereby causing the rumors to fly, but they seemed to have no such feelings, saying instead that it felt like such a weight had been lifted to have her gone and they were so relieved for the cats, and they said this in the manner of people who really were relieved, and Natsumi just gave a noncommittal, right, yes, in response, but it was undeniable that she, too, felt a sense of relief.

Chapter Seven – Female Friends

HER HUSBAND ALSO played the video games on the NES that the kids were so crazy about, arguing that they were surprisingly good for relieving stress, and said that since their children were growing up to live in the internet age, in the future they would use computers as a matter of course, and therefore, it made sense if they did their gaming on the computer to begin with, not on a console that plugged into the TV, but the kids had to keep up with the other children, which meant they wanted to play the games that everyone else in their respective classes were playing, and of course they didn't understand what their father was talking about, but that didn't stop them from getting carried away in the belief that although Mom didn't know the first thing about games, Dad understood and was on their side, and as a rule Natsumi loathed the hysterical high-pitched melodies made up of those ludicrously monotonous electronic noises, and when she was feeling frazzled before her period, the sound of this beeping would make the very innermost chamber of her head throb, and she'd develop a nauseous feeling in her chest. Once her period began, her irritation eased, and the noise of the NES would blend in with the hysterical racket from the TV and all the other kinds of daily clamors, so that it was no longer just that particular isolated irritant, and it wasn't as if she'd been actually diagnosed with premenstrual syndrome, but then the doctor whom she'd been seeing since she was a child was a woman who treated complaints from every branch of medicine including gynecology, internal medicine, pediatrics, and neurology, if you came down with a cold she would tell you to wrap yourself up in blankets and stay in bed, not to watch TV or read, if you got a bad stomachache from overeating she would tell you to avoid foods like gyōza and hamburgers and to eat plain udon, she'd give you just three days' worth of medicine and no injections, and even if all that was excusable, when you went to her with bad period pain she would say, the pain you're experiencing feels worse because you resent your period, spouting the kind of outdated sexist dogma that would definitely not be voiced to a patient complaining of any kind of pain other than period pain, and would prescribe only painkillers and tranquilizers, and as far as Natsumi's reading went, it seemed that ultimately most gynecologists thought the same, going by the understanding that whether the subject at hand was period pain or menopause it was just a matter of grinning and bearing it for a while, it was clear that it would pass naturally in time, and what was crucial was your zest for life, approaching things with a positive attitude, or in other words, your state of mind was the most important thing, apparently it all boiled down to that, and maybe that was true in a sense, but it seemed as though that was the prevailing attitude, at least the school nurse at her public middle school had been the same, and even the nurse at the private girls' high school she'd attended had said to them, at your age you shouldn't be using tampons, and Setchan had been outraged and said that advice came out of an internalization of the phallocentric idea that the vagina was a sacred place designed only for the penis to enter and for babies to emerge, and that accordingly women—let alone "intact" young girls—shouldn't put other objects in there, announcing that she had no intention of going anywhere near those diaper-like things, and using tampons without any compunction, and there was a group of girls in the class who would gossip about it in hushed voices as if totally scandalized by the whole affair, saying—in a way that qualified neither quite as criticism nor admiration—that *virgins didn't use tampons*, but when Natsumi, who had begun using tampons after being encouraged to do so by Setchan, said that, putting the issue of period pain aside, it was no exaggeration to claim that in being liberated from the misery of those napkins that you stuck, or rather, *applied* between your thighs, and that thick, heady smell of warm blood and discharge, and period underwear, her life had been changed, Setchan told her that, upon discovering that her daughter was using tampons, her mother had said to her, you, using these kinds of things, honestly! I don't know what's next, what on earth have you been getting up to, and began to interrogate her as if it were a box of condoms she'd found in her desk, and they'd gotten into an argument, and she went on and on about how inconsiderate I was, it was beyond belief, blah, blah, blah, as she recounted the tale Setchan had grown irate and said, stupid old hag, I wanted to *purge her* and *lynch her*, using the jargon that had become popular after the United Red Army incident, and Natsumi, also, had her box of Tampax discovered by her mother, who'd said, dear me, are these yours? it's usually only married women who use these, you must be very brave, the astonishment in her voice laced with malice, so that Natsumi had felt she was being treated as a loose woman, and the two of them had gotten so angry with the conservative attitude of their mothers and female teachers that construed menstruation and vaginas and sex as dirty and impure, and just remembering it now was enough to rile her up all over again, but in terms of her period, there was no doubt that the dull constricting ache in her lower back, which felt as though she were wearing two pairs of jeans on top of each other, and the headaches and irritations had grown worse these last two years, so she began to think about what they said about menopause in the magazine and newspaper articles on the topic that she would read whenever she stumbled across one because she figured that every woman went through it at some point, and started imagining how, during menopause, the headaches and the feeling of irritation that seemed to bounce around and reverberate inside her head would go on for longer than with PMS, which would sometimes make her feel vaguely anxious. Although no, the feeling that it evoked was maybe less one of anxiety and more a sense of unfairness, yes, perhaps that's a better description, she thought, aware of the stretched sensation in her face and hands that grew bloated during her period, and at times like these, she really wanted to toss everything else aside and sleep the entire day, but another part of her felt that it wasn't really right to do that, and she would end up feeling sick and tired of everything, and wind up totally exhausted.

As far as she could tell, her mother didn't really seem to get that way, although there was one occasion, around her fiftieth birthday, when she developed two varicose veins the size of pinky fingers sticking out from her left calf, and took a bit of a neurotic turn, was unable to sleep at night, thought about what would happen if something similar developed inside her brain and then burst, and that was the time when Natsumi's brother, who was four years younger than her, had taken a year off and postponed his entrance exams for university, and her mother had said, if something like that happened I might drop dead on the spot (I'd much prefer that), or else I might become paralyzed on one side of my body and lose the ability to speak (that would be terrible, who would take care of me then? there's no way your father could manage), but in any case I thought that I should at least write a will (I'm not concerned about whether or not it's legally valid), and had started jotting down all kinds of things in her notepad as drafts for what she wanted to tell the remaining family members, and quite possibly one of the reasons that the project had, inevitably, been quietly shelved was that Natsumi's brother had gotten into a university in Kyoto, and thinking about how her mother had seemed to feel that she now had a good excuse to stay in Kyoto and do a bit of sightseeing, and, saying that she was helping him with apartment hunting and then with the move, had ended up staying in Kyoto from the end of March through to the middle of May, and when she returned, it was as if nothing had ever happened, made that line of reasoning seem more probable, and when Natsumi yelled at her children in a hysterical tone of voice, saying, that's enough now! how many times have I told you not to do it when Mom has a headache! she imagined she made for quite a sight, with her face all puffed up and her temples twitching from her migraine, which got her thinking that the flat, monotonous life of the housewife—with all its set routines and its absence of change that somehow took an overwhelming toll on the spirit—really did deprive her of any kind of emotional space, and she knew that these feelings were of course tied up with the knowledge that the dinner for the group of the six of them who had been classmates at her private all-girls' high school for the first and second years, who couldn't exactly be called a close-knit group but somehow all got along well enough, and who had stayed in touch with one another, even in the third year of school when they were divided into different classes based on what they planned to do after, even after entering university, although they didn't necessarily meet up often, was coming up next week, and among that group of six former classmates Natsumi was the only housewife, and when she realized that how this made her feel was small, or somehow inferior, this thought piled on top of the irritability and the buzzing anxiety that made her throat tingle and the headache and the stomachache caused by her PMS, and she felt like she alone was losing out, and grew even more irritated and riled up by her husband, and recalling that she'd originally wanted to have a daughter, she'd feel dissatisfied by the fact that both her kids were boys, and whether it was at elementary school or kindergarten, all the Parents' Association stuff was pretty much assured to leave her feeling sick and tired of everything, once a month at kindergarten there was a "Mom's Homemade Snack Day," which meant being around the mothers of all the kids with their stupid trendy names like Risa and Juri and Asaka and Seiji and Yuta and Daichi, even if making snacks like yogurt jelly, cookies, sweet potatoes, pumpkin manjū, and Swiss-style fritters was maybe not the worst thing, and the group leader was a mother who prided herself on her talents in the kitchen so all Natsumi needed to do was leave the cooking to her, to look impressed by the fruits of that woman's culinary labors as she laid out the plates, and, of the ten mothers in that group, seven were housewives, little Tomoko's dad was a university teacher and a translator while her mom worked in the PR department of a food manufacturing company so it was her dad, his working hours being more flexible, who came to Mom's Homemade Snack Day, and he wasn't bad looking, and had dyed his longish, silky hair a chestnut color, so he was the focus of lots of attention, and when he said things like, shouldn't we change the name of Mom's Homemade Snack Day if I'm taking part, the delight among the teachers and the mothers was palpable, and Juri's mother, whose husband apparently ran a restaurant in Ginza, had said to Natsumi, I see that Tomoko takes after her mother, implying that neither Tomoko nor her mother were very good looking, and honestly, there's no shortage of bitchy women in this world. Even in talking about something totally unremarkable, some coincidental connection between people, like the fact that Mrs. Matsumoto and Mr. Takada's wife had been in the same year at university, yes, she commissioned a few pieces from me back when she was an editor so I know her well, oh, so you're friends are you, even during those kinds of utterly unremarkable conversations she could tell that everyone was watching him out of the corner of their eyes because the situation so closely resembled how, back at her girls' school, people had surreptitiously surveyed the young male teachers at all times, it's just, well, I mean, it's the dumbest thing, making cakes with those kinds of people, she said to her husband, who replied in a way, which, speaking metaphorically, resembled talking while leisurely plucking out his nose hairs, so if I were to join in this cake making, then I'd be the focus of everyone's attention too, so she replied huffily, no, in Mr. Takada's case it's because he's good looking, it's not like any old man will do, to which her husband said, having apparently put two and two together, oh, I see, it's like how Masakazu Tamura is so popular among middle-aged women, so Natsumi said, I'm not sure about "middle-aged women," the moms at Aoba Kindergarten are mostly younger than I am, some of them are in their twenties, to which her husband said, ohhh, I see, so they go around wearing miniskirts and all that, now I *really* want to try out this cake-making thing, and then he cackled at his own corny, idiotic locker-room joke in a way that made her feel truly revolted, and in the last two or three days, there had been a series of disagreeable things like that happening, all just minor occurrences that individually wouldn't have affected her too much, really, but all those little things—rushing to pick up the phone while she was doing the laundry to find it was a wrong number, and the person on the other end said, it's Murayama here, and when she asked, Mr. Murayama from where, might I ask, the person on the other end didn't apologize for getting the wrong number but instead said, in a way that seemed to suggest that it was her fault for picking up the phone, that's strange, who are you? in a croaky voice, the kind of voice that old people developed when they had phlegm permanently lodged in their throats, the sort unique to men who'd gone on speaking in an imperious way to people around them for decades (and he phoned back three times, leaving a three-minute gap between each call), and she'd failed to notice a red origami creature in her younger boy's shorts pocket (when she asked afterward she discovered they'd made frogs at kindergarten) before she put it in the machine and all of the clothes along with it had been stained pink, and his shorts were now splattered with red splotches, and the whole load of washing was covered in minuscule shreds of ripped-up paper, and a venetian-glass cup with white diagonal stripes suspended in see-through glass (that she'd bought on a weeklong travel package to Florence, Venice, and Milan that she'd been on back in her working days) had jumped out of her fingers that were slippery with dish soap and struck her husband's teacup that was lying in the sink (which was the creation of his high school friend Yamasaki who had left his office job to become a ceramicist, and she didn't know what this particular style of pottery that he made was called, but it was very crude looking and she couldn't see what it had going for it at all) and had broken, which had made her mad with frustration because she wished it had been the other way round—started to add up, they made her increasingly sensitive, that was the cycle she was trapped in, and her husband said to her hesitantly, in an attentive, even fawning tone of voice, going out with your friends for the first time in ages will cheer you up, won't it, and then added, out of that group you're the most beautiful, so you can at least get dressed up and remind yourself of that, right? to which she responded, if you're going to flatter people then you could at least flatter them properly, why is it that the only compliments that you're capable of giving are the stingy, small-minded kind, if you came out and said to me, I think you're beautiful, then even if I found it contrived and it annoyed me, I'd still think, well at least you alone still think that about me, and that wouldn't be a bad feeling to have, and we could both feel better as a result, what I don't understand is why you have to go and add "out of that group," it's made me uncomfortable before, the way you speak about them as if they were such an ugly bunch, she said, growing more and more critical, and even as she was saying this she realized that she was finding fault just for the sake of it but still she couldn't stop herself, and even if the *oh crap* face her husband made when he realized he'd gone and put his foot in it with something he'd said with the best of intentions irritated her even more, that wasn't because she thought her husband was a big-footed bumbling idiot (he was five foot nine with size 9 ½ feet which probably placed him right on the cusp of being big footed)—although, of course, there were insensitive elements to him—but because her anger toward him stemmed from her insecurities about being a housewife, and that realization brought on a burst of self-loathing.

In an advertisement for a women's magazine in that morning's newspaper she saw the words *Is Being a Wife and a Mother Stopping You from Doing What You Want to Do?* parading in great big letters across the page, and in slightly smaller print, *Do you find that your days get eaten up by the constant struggle to keep up with the housework and childcare, and you end up putting all the things you wanted to do and the dreams for the future you once had on hold? When you think about yourself, are you sometimes visited by the lonely feeling that the world is moving on without you, or a sense of panic about whether you're good enough as you are? If so, this issue can change all that. We showcase the women who have made the things they want in life happen. Their vitality speaks volumes—it is possible to both be a housewife and realize your dreams! It's time to stop feeding yourself the excuse that nothing can be done for the moment. Now it's your turn to start something new,* and reading this, Natsumi thought, leaving aside the question of whether it counted as "both being a housewife and realizing your dreams," it was an unshakable fact that an overwhelming number of housewives did *something,* and it was also definitely the case that the ones who did apply themselves to something seemed somehow full of vitality—no, that was an affected way of putting it, but suffice to say that they seemed to be having fun and enjoying life, and among her friends and acquaintances who were also mothers was a woman who'd started making Kamakura-bori lacquerware when she'd hit menopause and had put on a solo exhibition of her efforts, and a woman who took thread dyed with tints extracted from plants and trees and wove it into fabric that she used to make bags, shawls, and gilets and so on, which she sold—and at a handsome price—in a small shop that she'd set up by converting a room in her house in a very ordinary residential district, and a woman who, inspired by the the dyeing woman, had renovated her house and, drawing on her interest in making cakes, which had been her passion for many years, opened a baking school there, and a woman who'd made use of her spacious home to open up a handmade udon and kaiseki restaurant with a friend, and a woman who'd gotten her real estate license and set up a real estate agency by the Keiō Subway Line, and both her mother and her mother-in-law in Nagano had several friends who had taken lessons at one of the nationwide chain of kimono-dressing schools and gotten their own teaching qualifications, and Mrs. Nakamura the Crazy Cat Lady also taught twice a week at a kimono-dressing school, and a group of housewives from thirty-six households in Natsumi's complex, the eighteen apartments in Block A together with the eighteen in Block B, which was of identical construction across the courtyard, had gotten together to run classes out of their own apartments in things like knitting, embroidery, flower arranging, patchwork, kimekomi doll making, cooking, metal carving, incense appreciation ceremony, calligraphy, and Ogasawara etiquette, while other housewives rented shops in separate locations, where they ran catering and delivery services for parties, or sold tableware or secondhand goods, or ran cafés, and all of them seemed to have a firm sense of what they actually wanted to pursue, and it seemed as though the housewives with no hobbies who had nothing they particularly wanted to do were in the minority. There was no way of knowing the real reason why, whether this was in fact what she really wanted to do or whether she'd despaired of this life in which it seemed as though everybody was supposed to have *something they really wanted to do*, but the "educated" guess of Mrs. Hirano, from whom she heard about the incident, went as follows: there had been someone living in this building who had a nervous breakdown or had at least become mentally unwell after her husband had taken a lover, and committed suicide by jumping from the roof, which was, in fact, very rare, people tended to jump from a building other than the one they were living in, out of consideration for their families, or at least that was what she'd heard from Mrs. Nakamura, whose son was a lawyer, and so, Mrs. Hirano said, the woman who committed suicide must've wanted to get back at the husband she was leaving, and it had been such a tragedy because she'd landed on one of the two large white-and-blue striped parasols by the children's pool in the courtyard, and the rib of the parasol had broken and stabbed her, Mrs. Hirano said, it was after midnight one August night, there was the bluish-white light from the moth traps around the pool, and I expect you must have glanced down and seen it, so you know, but the reflected light from the fluorescent lamps on the ceilings of the corridors on every floor floats hazily on the surface of the pool, and, I mean, if you were going to kill yourself by jumping off a building, would you do it at night, or during the day? Mrs. Hirano said with a pensive expression, and then, without waiting for Natsumi's response, said, I think if it was me, it'd have to be at night, if it was daytime you'd be able to see the ground, you'd see everything too clearly, I'd be too frightened, and then she said, although thinking about it, in those sorts of films starring those tough-guy detectives, there are often scenes where they try to talk people down from the ledge on top of buildings in broad daylight, my guess is they want to jump during the day so that someone might notice them and stop them, she said, nodding, and Natsumi, looking down at the surface of the pool uneasily, said, but would anybody really kill themselves just because their husband started cheating? I can't really understand that, she said, cocking her head, and Mrs. Hirano said, well, yes, you may be right, I suppose, that probably wouldn't be the only thing, would it, that alone wouldn't be enough to make you do it, she said nodding, I suppose we don't really know the reason, but it is true that her husband was having an affair, I'm sure of that.

And afterward, Mrs. Hirano went on, something else happened that wasn't as shocking as the suicide, a different person was rumored to be working as the recruiter for a secret housewife prostitution agency, it's okay to tell you now, and as she said this, she lowered her voice and held up her left hand to the side of her mouth in an overt "I'm telling you a secret" gesture, so that Natsumi, too, felt drawn into the clandestine nature of the conversation and leaned in farther toward Mrs. Hirano, who was considerably shorter than her, and responded to what she was saying with a look of great interest, saying in a slightly hushed voice, really, in this block? thinking all the while that if someone saw them standing there by the azalea bush in the courtyard talking like this they would assume without any doubt whatsoever that they were gossiping about someone else in the building, but then she thought, well, so what, let them think that, while Mrs. Hirano said, it's okay to tell you about it, isn't it, now that she doesn't live here anymore, and nodded knowingly, and suddenly it clicked with Natsumi and she said, ohhh, and Mrs. Hirano said, yes, yes, exactly, and nodded again as if to say, trust an insightful person like yourself to understand so quickly, and then carried on, there was one woman who had gotten quite friendly with her, and one day she came out and asked her if she'd like to go on a date with one of her male friends, just a very casual thing, for a little change of scenery, they're all very kind and easy to be around, very pleasant people, I've introduced them to several of the wives in this building, and apparently the woman realized instantly what she was being asked to do, and began to gradually distance herself from this woman, she said she didn't do anything dramatic, Mrs. Hirano said, but that woman's husband was in securities or real estate or something financial, and my guess is that when the bubble era ended, she felt like she had to do something to contribute financially as well, if you use your apartment as an office then you don't have to pay any extra tax, and there aren't any added expenses, so you can take home all the earnings, I imagine, she said, so Natsumi said, yes, I imagine so, and remembered how, when she was in middle school or high school, so sometime around the beginning of the seventies, everyone had been talking about the issue of housewife prostitution, and at that time she'd read an article, probably in the *Asahi Journal* that her father subscribed to—or was it *Fujin Kōron*—which had painted a picture of housewives who weren't very young anymore and seemed disillusioned by life, dressed in the kind of attire you'd expect to find on someone you'd encounter at the local shop with a basket on one arm buying ingredients for dinner, who would instead stand in the dark spots under the girders near train stations and solicit customers, and who had told the journalist how, with mortgage repayments and mounting school tuition fees, they were only just scraping by, or their husbands had lost their jobs after the Nixon shock and they wanted to be able to feed their growing children meat for at least one meal of the day, and then she remembered how Matsumoto, who had been part of the Humanities Club in high school, which was rumored to have been founded by a former student called so-and-so who had been part of the Zenkyōtō antigovernment protests, had said that prostitution existed because there were men who paid money for sex, to which Uchida and Yukari, with whom she was good friends, had said to one another, how much would you do it for, I wouldn't do it for 100,000 yen, but if it was 1,000,000 yen a pop then maybe I'd think about it, and Natsumi, Matsumoto, Setchan, and Momoko had stopped speaking to the two of them as a result, and it occurred to her that the next time she saw Yukari she would bring up the subject, ask her if she still thought the same, comment that her rates would probably have gone down by now, and generally be cruel to her, and then she remembered something she'd heard from Mrs. Asakura who'd been taking screenplay-writing lessons at the Culture Center, about how in the apartment block she'd lived in before there'd been a woman who'd jumped from the balcony of her third-floor apartment, but ended up with only a broken leg, and who'd apparently told Mrs. Asakura afterward that she herself couldn't think of any reason for committing suicide, she'd just been hanging out her laundry when she'd happened to look down, and had the sensation of being sucked toward the ground, feeling that it would be easy to jump, and she remembered also how her Yukigaya uncle had done the same thing a lot when he was younger, sometimes he'd get away with just a sprain, but his mother had worried all the time that one day he'd mistakenly end up dying when he had no intention of killing himself, or so Natsumi's mother had said.

As far as "the thing she really wanted to do" went, at any particular point in time there'd always been *something*, from early childhood onward, but when she thought about those *somethings*, they were all in the vein of becoming a pianist or a ballerina or a fashion designer, things that she'd alighted upon casually by reading the same shōjo manga as all the other girls in her class, and of course she never went as far as taking lessons in any of those things, and when playing the school upright pianos that the girls in her class shared between the twenty of them, four girls to each piano, she never once felt that she wanted one herself, and when in the third year of elementary school she'd had a writing assignment about what she wanted to be when she grew up—she couldn't remember now if it was in Japanese class or general studies—she'd written that she wanted to either become her Yukigaya uncle or own a bird shop, and the reason that she'd written about the bird shop was because the daruma parakeet Da-chan she'd had as a pet at the time was such a tame, clever, and adorable creature, and she'd felt that living surrounded by little birds like that might be nice, and her Yukigaya uncle was her mother's brother, three years older than her mother, who had died two years later, he'd gone funny in the head after leaving university and had spent some time in a psychiatric hospital, and had subsequently never found a steady job and idled around at his parents' house instead, reading books until dawn, sleeping during the day, and taking the dog for walks, and so on, and when Natsumi and her brother went to visit he would always be very nice to them and play with them, and it had seemed to Natsumi that not having a demanding job like regular adults was a wonderful thing, and so she'd written that she wanted to grow up to be like him, but of course she wasn't thinking that she wanted to fly down to earth or take off from a high spot like a winged bird, and her homeroom teacher Mrs. Yamaguchi who'd just come back from maternity leave seemed to have misconstrued what she was trying to say, because she wrote in the margin of Natsumi's Kokuyo notebook, *I see that you love your kind uncle who plays with you and those adorable little birds! Would you like to be a kindergarten teacher when you grow up?* and Natsumi had no idea what she meant, or why she would want to become a kindergarten teacher, and was confused by the comment, and when it came to "things that she didn't want to do but had to do regardless," well there were tons of them, and none of them were the grand sorts of things that anybody would call dreams or major ambitions, they were just things she wanted to do at that particular time in that particular place, I've spent my life up until now doing those kinds of things, she thought. She wasn't a particularly handy type, but she'd knitted six and a half sweaters—if you counted the one she'd started knitting for her husband three years ago and still hadn't finished—including children's ones, by consulting a manual, and she baked cakes, not very well but passably, and she'd tried out both embroidery and patchwork, but felt that she didn't want to involve herself any further with them, and so on her CV she wrote that her hobby was reading, and there'd been a time when that was the truth.

They'd arranged to meet at six on Saturday at the French-style Japanese restaurant in Matsumizaka, which Setchan, who'd been once before, said wasn't expensive, and also didn't seem like the kind of place that would've been a hot date spot for young executives back in the bubble economy era, the restaurant was generally laid-back with a comparatively large number of female customers, the sort of place where at any given time two people there will be wearing Issey Miyake's Pleats Please, Setchan said, and so after a lot of consideration, Natsumi decided to wear her milky-tea-colored silk blouse after all, with a pair of black wool pants and black calfskin pumps, which she complemented with a necklace she'd bought in the accessories section of Tokyu Department Store, of a slightly unusual design consisting of six thin matte gold chains, and also decided to take along the shoulder bag that she'd chosen for her birthday the year before last and asked her husband to reimburse her for, and when she was all ready to go out, her husband, who was preparing to cook okonomiyaki on the hot-plate, said, oh, very cool, that really suits you, and the kids, who were in high spirits because they were having okonomiyaki for dinner, mimicked their dad and said, very cool! and Natsumi cocked her chin, and said, mmhm-hm, then struck a pose, and said, right? and left the house.

The concept behind this place is not to splurge on the decor and tableware, allowing diners to enjoy the food and wine they serve at reasonable prices, the building is the house of the owner which they've refurbished so there's no rent to pay either, explained Matsumoto, who had given up her job as an editor and was now working as a freelance writer, and who had been the one to recommend the restaurant in the first place, and then she said, it's been such a long time since we all got together like this, it must be almost two years, right? and let out a sigh, and then Setchan and Momoko turned up, and then after a while Uchida and Yukari appeared and sat down at the table.

Momoko, whose mother—with whom she'd been living for ten years—had been in the hospital for two months back in June, seemed exhausted, she spoke of a newspaper advertisement for *Croissant* magazine that said, spread out over two lines, the top line in large print and the one below in slightly smaller print, *To keep your feelings and soul youthful, you need to nourish your mind! Have you read any books that captured your heart recently?* and though she hadn't bought the magazine itself, she said, I thought it was stupid, what's with "feelings and soul" as a combination, and using such a domestic word like "nourish" too, but it's also true that I haven't read a book from cover to cover recently, and when I think about it, that's not because I haven't had the time to read a book, I've been busy looking after my mother, but if I'd really wanted to read one or needed to read one, then I'm sure I'd manage to have squeezed in some reading time somehow, at the end of the day the truth is that I just didn't want to read, I don't think there's any point pretending I really wanted to read but I simply couldn't, she said, and Natsumi replied that she thought that was exactly right, but Matsumoto and Yukari, who had jobs where they might have been expected to read books, didn't give much of a reaction, and Setchan offered a pitying expression, and Uchida (whose maiden name was Hashizume) talked about how her husband, who worked in the sales department of a company that made aluminum sash windows, had taken a week off work and gone to volunteer in Kobe, to help with the aftermath of the earthquake, to which Setchan said, they're putting up so many new buildings there, I guess sash windows must be in high demand, nice to be able to kill two birds with one stone! at which Uchida looked huffy and said, he went as a volunteer, not as a salesman, and thus the tension between them that had existed since high school showed its face for a moment, but then Setchan took out from her brown leather briefcase a photocopy of the essay about the Kineo Kuwabara exhibition she'd promised to give to Natsumi when they'd spoken on the phone, holding it out and saying, I'll give this to you before I forget, and Natsumi answered, okay, it'll be the first thing I've read in a while, and that meal of theirs, the first they'd had together in so long, had a strange mood about it, and when the amicable middle-aged waitress who brought over the oshibori moist towels for them to wipe their hands with before eating warned them that the towels were hot, and unfolded them, allowing them to cool slightly, before handing them over to each woman, Uchida received hers with a slightly haughty demeanor, or at least, a demeanor that suggested that she was very much used to being served by other people and thought nothing of it, and then said, speaking of oshibori, leaving a pause before continuing, I bumped into Yokobori not long ago, she said, naming someone who'd been in the same year at the same women's university as Natsumi and Yukari, so everyone looked at one another, and Natsumi spat out angrily, what kind of a connection is that? what's the connection between oshibori and Yokobori? but Uchida didn't seem fazed at all, saying that she'd run into Yokobori, whom she hadn't seen since Yokobori had gotten divorced and gone back home to live with her parents in Hakata, on the platform at Shin-Kyoto Station, and though there hadn't been the time to really catch up she'd seemed well, and was wearing what looked like a Bulgari ring, so I guess she got remarried, I didn't have time to ask, she said, to which Matsumoto said, huh, figures you'd know it was Bulgari at a single glance, you and I have always been of a different class, in both school and society, but even this mean-spirited comment didn't elicit a reaction from Uchida, who took out a newspaper clipping of a book review from her bag, saying to Setchan, he was saying that this book contains everything you need to know about his concept for living and he wants people to read it, putting it on the table in front of her, and Matsumoto snatched it up saying, what's this? *My Philosophy for Living* … ? *In this book the author, an architect and a poet, likens life to a voyage at sea where the weather is not always temperate, and where we at times find ourselves stricken by fierce storms, rocked and jolted around in turbulent waves. For this reason, he postulates, one needs a home to serve as a reliable vessel, and provides guidance to readers about the architectural details of their home from this perspective.* (Here Matsumoto snorted.) *Homes need to be sufficiently robust to provide shelter to their human inhabitants both structurally and psychologically, but if they are too imposing in nature, they can't be of help during times of spiritual storm.* (And so it goes on, Matsumoto said, and then continued.) *In this book, the author lays out his faith in an aggressive belief in cocooning, identifying the ship drifting through the void of the cosmos as both weapon in confronting the universe and vessel for the soul, representing as it does the root of our "individuality,"* it says! It makes me think of that Walt Disney series *Lost in Space,* she said contemptuously, and Setchan said to Uchida, cocooning isn't really my thing at all, you're better off asking someone else, there are architects whose concepts for living are a much better match with this philosophy, and it was obvious from the way she spoke that she was fed up, and when she tasted the strange concoction of lightly mashed taro seasoned with dashi stock—or was it some kind of soup?—and sprinkled with caviar that'd been brought out in tiny dishes with a blue-and-white design she pulled an unconvinced expression, and when the dish of daikon stewed in aigamo duck soup with a piece of foie gras perched on top was served she looked even more dissatisfied—the others said, in front of Matsumoto, that it had a slightly unusual taste but it was really good—which seemed to hasten the souring of the whole event, and the fact that, aside from Uchida and herself, everyone else was wearing a casual outfit became a source of regret to Natsumi on multiple fronts, and though she managed not to get any food stains on what she was wearing, it was a warm and clammy day for that time of the year and her armpits grew sweaty, leaving patches on her blouse (she'd neglected to shave her armpits, with the thought that it was long-sleeved so she'd be fine to do so, but she shouldn't have!) and the idea that she'd have to take the blouse to the cleaner's after just one wear was another thing that irritated her.

They didn't drink like fishes as they had back in the days when they'd knocked back margaritas and whiskies, and instead everyone went home at an intermediary stage of drunkenness, poised between drinking properly and not drinking at all, and she forgot about the photocopy Setchan had given her, so that it was not until a while later that she actually read it.

WARPING AND ETHICS

So moderate and comfortable in its design is the Setagaya Art Museum—the creation of the same architect responsible for the Fukiage Imperial Palace—that it more closely resembles a hotel built with the intimate feel of a second home such as those found before the Second World War in the resort towns of Hakone or Karuizawa than it does any art museum, and if, hypothetically speaking, a single woman of thirty-one or thirty-two who worked in the advertising department of a company responsible for the distribution of Western films, or a twenty-six-year-old woman who worked a desk job at a trading conglomerate (who had not entered the company on the career track) and was engaged to be married to a colleague currently working for the Côte d'Ivoire or Amman branch of the same company ended up having an affair with someone whom I don't have the space here to imagine and consider how she might have met, then, that being the case, the museum is exactly the kind of place that a novelist would conceive of them being invited along on a date to by the copy editor of a weekly magazine, aged somewhere between thirty-seven and forty-five, or the director (or else producer) of a culture program on TV who hadn't been involved in the recent staged documentary scandal but was nevertheless unable to think about the issue as one entirely unrelated to him, as a location where they could enjoy a cultural experience together.

With its verdigris roof and pale-brown tiles, its monastery-like cloisters and simple wooden construction,

the building casts tasteful contemporary Japanese bourgeois conservatism in an appealing light, and truly does
have something about it that spurs the imagination,
causing one to dream up those kinds of hackneyed sce-
narios, whereby the copy editor, or the director, finding
out that the title of the Nobuyoshi Araki and Kineo Kuwabara exhibition was LOVE YOU TOKYO!, and that it
was at the Setagaya Art Museum—which was just *such a
nice spot*—decided to invite his lover along. The woman
working in the advertising department of the company
distributing Western films had, while studying abroad
in Paris, visited the *Japon des avant-gardes* exhibition at
the Centre Pompidou with an American journalist, and
hence knew of Kuwabara's photography—the American journalist, whom she'd met at the *cinématèque*, had
been a Japanophile, and had said to her that Kuwabara's
photographs had a way of capturing the world that was
far more dynamic than that of Ozu, and which reminded
him of Mikio Naruse, that the two showcased the beauty
of the Japanese people in an analogous way, but she had
not seen a single one of Naruse's films—and she had
also, of course, heard of Araki. The office lady at the trading company had never heard of Kineo Kuwabara, but
the photographer who went by the moniker ARAKI was
famous (she'd seen him once on a late-night TV show),
and she knew that his photographs were, to borrow the
phrase of a girl in the same year as her at college, "dirty
photos," but according to the director, whose second
daughter had just entered kindergarten, they weren't *just*
"dirty photos," but enough of a big deal that they would
someday have to feature his photographs, including his
nudes, on the *Sunday Art Museum* program that screened

on the national TV channel where he worked and invite Kōtarō Iizawa or some other big-name art critic along as a guest, and even if you ascribed the way that Kōtarō Iizawa had talked about Araki's photographs in terms of the Melancholic, that paradigmatic concept of the nineteenth century psyche, to Iizawa being a photography critic and therefore uneducated, you couldn't overlook the fact that people like Gen'ichiro Takahashi, Taeko Tomioka, and Yūko Tanaka admitted that, unlike the stereotypically beautiful nudes by Kishin Shinoyama, which everybody felt that they'd seen somewhere before, but which lacked any kind of contemporary sense of relevance or provocation, Araki's nudes revealed a certain truth about the times in which we are living, or at least, that was what the director had explained when they were sitting in the Shiseido Parlour in Laforet Harajuku, and the fact that he clearly inhabited a totally different world from her fiancé who worked in a trading firm (an airmail letter had arrived from him yesterday saying that the humidity in the Côte d'Ivoire made it feel "like a steam bath") made him attractive to her, but when he spoke, the top left-hand corner of his mouth would jerk upward, and his jaw would jut out to the left at the same time, which was another reason why she didn't want to go with him to a hotel.

As suggested by its whimsical-sounding title, LOVE YOU TOKYO!, it's Asia's sordid international metropolis, shape-shifting dynamically as it is ravaged and consumed, that forms the subject of the exhibition—a city that is perhaps well suited to have its name written not in kanji, as is standard, but rather in the katakana script used for foreign words, as in the Japanese title to the exhibition—which presents the work of two photographers born and bred in the city (in the same Taito Ward, in fact, though different parts of it) a generation apart, like father and child, taken over the half-century period between 1930 and 1993 and arranged to give visitors a sense of navigating their way through a convoluted maze of narrow alleyways.

The two young, unmarried women didn't know the hit song "Love You Tokyo" that had been sung by Akira Kurosawa and Los Primos, but the copy editor and the TV-channel director knew it, and in fact, when men of the former's age would sing their karaoke renditions of songs such as "Karajishi Botan" and Yuzo Kayama's "Itsumade mo," brimming with emotion, the copy editor, who was born in 1947, would frequently counter with "Love You Tokyo," or else Linda Yamamoto's "Komacchauna," and enjoyed pulling the wool over the eyes of the young women who happened to be around by pretending that this Akira Kurosawa was *that* Akira Kurosawa, but he hadn't been born in Tokyo (neither, in fact, had the director), and as for the two women, the advertising lady was a second-generation Tokyoite, her father and his siblings the first to have been born in the capital, while the woman in the trading conglomerate's great-great-grandfather had been a member of the southern Satsuma clan, born a low-ranking samurai and serving with the clan's forces, and since her grandfather's generation, her family had been bureaucrats for the Ministry of Economy, Trade and Industry, living in Tokyo's Suginami Ward.

With its verdigris roof and its tiles in the something-or-other style, the Setagaya Art Museum has a more or less identical design concept to the Imperial Palace, and when you think about that in reference to modern Europe, where art museums such as Florence's Uffizi, the Louvre after the French Revolution, and the Hermitage after the Russian Revolution were a part of the history of Enlightenment philosophy, in the sense that they served as spaces where the collections of the imperial or royal families and the aristocracy were made available to the public, then it's as if the Setagaya Art Museum serves as the antithesis of that, it's assimilated with the residential spaces of the Emperor, do you see what I mean, in present-day Heisei era Japan the public space of the art museum follows the example of the Imperial Palace, the director said, simply parroting the lines that an art critic he'd been at university with (whose uncle was a historian specializing in the Annales school) had written in a magazine article, at which the woman with the desk job nodded as if struck by this observation, and said, it sort of feels like how the old Nara Hotel or the Hakone Fujiya Hotel would look if they were renovated.

Is this exhibition, in fact, an appropriate match for its ironic title LOVE YOU TOKYO! and the journalistic ring that it carries? Considering the words alone, it seems immediately obvious that the title's intended implication is that the warping of the photographers' feelings toward the supermetropolis of Tokyo imbues them with a criticality that allows them to function as love, and as we have in all likelihood understood Nobuyoshi Araki's photographic oeuvre as manifesting a criticality that stems from such warped feelings as directed toward numerous contemporary "issues" such as photography, the city, culture, sexual mores, and death, the fact of the exhibition being given this title, LOVE YOU TOKYO!, with the somewhat outdated flippant note it strikes, didn't make us feel remotely uneasy, and it is indeed possible to understand the notable lack of "I" within the phrase as simultaneously indicating the subsumption of the subject within the amorphous city of TOKYO, and as a linguistic simplification aligned with Nobuyoshi Araki signing his work ARAKI, to wit, a warped kind of critical coinage. We do get slightly sick of the fact that, standing in front of ARAKI's photos, we end up bringing to mind terms of infantile psychology like "warped."

That said, after taking a turn around the artificial alleyways erected in the gallery space that lead us through an entire half-century, visitors to the exhibition find that, at each of the turning points in those artificial alleys, it's the Kuwabara photographs that all eyes are drawn to, each of which, in exposing the limits of an Arakiesque criticality as they appeal by virtue of being real photographs, far transcend any of Araki's actual photos. Why might such a thing be happening? You could of course put it down simply to the difference in talent between the two and be done with it—and it should be hastily noted that the phrase "difference in talent" is being used here to indicate not a discrepancy in the presence or absence of talent, but rather to refer to an essential difference in the nature of the talent—but even by doing so, it's impossible to gloss over the cruelty of the way that the Arakiesque criticality in Nobuyoshi Araki's photographs is surpassed so overwhelmingly by the abundant joy found in the desirous gaze of Kineo Kuwabara's photographs.

Of course, the very nature of photography means something different to Kuwabara than it does to Araki, who is of Kuwabara's son's generation, and it also stands to reason that the material significance of Kuwabara's photos of the dancing girls in Asakusa is different from that of Araki's photographs of sex workers, and when we go to compare the complex-yet-simple surprise, sadness, humor, and compassion-filled affection we find in the photograph Kuwabara took of the four elementary school boys lost in thought in the back seat of a bus in the 1970s with one of Araki's photographs of children, taken with a lens that deliberately produces a grainy finish, and displaying a criticality toward contemporary society that derives from the sheer fact of their being photographs and therefore being so easily comprehensible as to verge on a form of defenselessness, we probably need to consider the era in which these two photographs are taken and perhaps reflect that the criticality of the photographer resides precisely in capturing his own era, and looking at the picture of Araki taken by Eiichirō Sakata that appears in the thick exhibition catalog for LOVE YOU TOKYO!, on what would be the back cover if you were to pick up the book and read from right to left, and at his expression, which, leaving aside the round sunglasses and white moustache, is a mixture of diligence, kindness, and shyness, the viewer starts to doubt their own eyes, to wonder if this is really the same Araki as the one who appears among the "dirty photos" (to borrow the phrase used by the novelist Anna Ogino) that ARAKI took with the self-timer function, where he himself wears the same eerie, frozen expression of nervousness and distrust toward the photographer as his own subjects do, and to wonder also if the criticality found in Araki's photographs is actually more concerned with the identities of those people living out their lives within the contemporary city, highlighting the lies that at first glance appear as realities, and although we knew it all along, we end up reconfirming for ourselves that despite Araki's possession of the talents and diligence needed by someone who works as both journalist and critic, his work is really quite dull.

The camera, apparatus of the desirous gaze, is made up of a shutter released upon a scene which one feels certain can never be fully contained within a 35 mm frame by a finger that is determined to live in the present moment, full as that moment is of affection, curiosity, and regret toward all those people living through the world's uncontainable time and space. The determination, the hesitation, the joy and fear of the moment when the finger releases the shutter are not about any critical consistency of a journalistic nature, but rather *the ethics of the person holding the camera*, who, with the rapid movement of a finger, must make an instantaneous decision with that desirous gaze. Indeed, this dynamic ethics of photography is what makes possible the momentary interlocking of the finger on the shutter and the desirous gaze, an interlocking to which Kuwabara's photography—right up until his most recent work, *Afternoon Smiles* (1992)—owes its ability to move the viewer. The finer details of the fragile beauty and its sensuous glimmer that reside within the ethicality of such a photographer can very often be lost from the originals in the process of mass-producing them, similar to watching a film on videotape.

The field of photography, which evolved into a medium through the emergence of the distinction between *amateurs* and *experts*, that was in turn made possible by advances in development and printing technology and which then went on to give rise to *professional* and *fine-art photographers*, has thus accomplished in a flash the transition from commemorative albums for bourgeois families to grand symbol of printed media within popular consumerist society, and yet perhaps finds itself simultaneously fated, when within the nineteenth-century-style public exhibition space, to attest endlessly to the quality—i.e., the artistry—of its prints *as* prints.

Hmmmmmm, the woman working at the trading conglomerate said to the director. I dunno, but they seem kind of flat? Or tacky, or something? It's just a bunch of naked women, they're not really even very smutty, you see loads of photos like this in the weekly magazines, and on TV too, right? The director was at a loss for how to reply, mentioning pubic hair and Gen'ichiro Takahashi's name and the contemporary criticality of Araki again, and the single young woman working in the advertising department of the company distributing Western films understood Kineo Kuwabara's photos far better now than when she'd seen them in Paris and felt moved by them, felt now, this guy is a true photographer, while Araki, who'd lived in and amid a Tokyo experiencing the schizophrenic flattening that accompanies modernization and has captured the symptoms of that disorder, is a diligent journalist, he's capturing in imagistic form the schizophrenic contemporary age where a girl from the sex industry and your wife's face as she dies appear the same to you, it's that pernicious brand of modernism known as realism, she said in the French restaurant that jutted out from the left wing of the Setagaya Art Museum with its pared-back interior design that reflected the taste of the Imperial Family, and the copy editor thought, as he remembered the photograph that showed a Shinjuku skyscraper at a diagonal angle, that the main theme of Araki's photography was quite possibly that of papering over the castration complex with sheer bravado.

Araki's photographs do not threaten our images of Tokyo, or of sex, and especially not of death. Because they are earnestly presented to us in the belief that they will challenge and complicate such images, his photographs deliver a comfortable shock, before stopping short and beginning to become flat. Through the value schema of contemporary criticism that construes the flattening of every kind of value as the unique feature of the contemporary age, Nobuyoshi Araki flattens himself into ARAKI. When Araki, whose photographs are surely taken as ironic depictions of the age, as described by Daniel J. Boorstin's *The Image: A Guide to Pseudo-Events in America*, which holds that the photographs that a tourist takes on their travels are flattened into the "experience" of the backpacking tour, is unable to transcend the ambiguity of the image, which is after all not so simple to achieve—what these photographs tell us is that neither

TOKYO nor Tokyo can be fully accommodated within the photographic image, and neither can middle-aged women, girls in the sex industry, faces at the moment of death, or sex—it is Kineo Kuwabara's photographs that place a bet with the ethics of the finger and the gaze on that apparatus known as the camera, turn to face the present time of the viewer, and speak for the power in the presence of those people living through this moment in time, this moment in space, which can only exist in this photograph. *We will not become flattened, even if we are captured on film.*

The title given to Kuwabara's most recent photo exhibition, *Afternoon Smiles* (1992), refers to the smiles of reconfirming, in the ethics of the finger and the gaze, a world—be that of Tokyo or TOKYO—that is not flattened by being accommodated within the frame, which flows over with the dynamism of time and life, and truly continues to expand. By sharing Kuwabara's smiles, we can find the conviction to live in this world.

THE IMMEDIACY OF THE LIGHT

Is the impression that the chunky, A5-sized book containing 735 photographs of Tokyo taken between 1934 and 1993 leaves on the reader, as the words on the belly band suggest, "a portrait of the unforgettable form taken by the great city of Tokyo captured across a period of sixty years" whereby "everything sparkles, thus illuminating what is to come with an indubitable glimmer"—is it, in other words, one that boils down to undisguised nostalgia?

Tokyo 1934–1993, while being a retrospective of the work of amateur photographer Kineo Kuwabara, also manifests an apparent editorial direction, which, in presenting this "portrait" of the unforgettable form taken by the great city of Tokyo captured across a period of sixty years," inevitably stirs up a sense of nostalgia for the changing face of the city.

The woman who was twenty-six and working a desk job at a trading conglomerate when she saw LOVE YOU TOKYO! at the Setagaya Art Museum in the summer of 1993 had subsequently left that firm, which had become a very difficult employer for someone past the age of twenty-six, and had taken up a job as an editor at a small publishing company, and in February of this year—having the previous winter already broken off her engagement with her fiancé, a colleague from the trading conglomerate working at its Côte d'Ivoire branch—had also split with the copy editor of a weekly magazine with whom she'd been having an affair, and was now dating a master's student three years her junior—a young film buff she'd met in Lisbon while on a trip she took after breaking off both her engagement and her affair, and which she thought about as, using the English words, her *sentimental journey*—although their relationship wasn't physical, they just occasionally went to the cinema and to restaurants, and this time too, he had asked her out, saying that they simply had to go and see a couple of films screening in the "Nippon Cinema Classics" program at the Tokyo International Film Festival.

Once the films were finished, over a meal at Sabatini, the woman had said, in the upcoming edition of our magazine, and the MA student had felt a slight sense of discomfort at her usage of the word "our" but didn't mention it, and when she quoted the title of the upcoming special feature, "Nostalgia: I Want to Go Back to That Day …" and discussed its contents, he couldn't stop himself from shooting her an incredulous look, and yet he'd proceeded nonetheless to hand her a copy of *Tokyo 1934–1993*, saying, this might be helpful to you, to which she said, with evident pleasure, oh, Kineo Kuwabara, I've seen an exhibition of his, and the MA student commented that of the two Mikio Naruse films they'd just seen, *The Girl in the Rumor* was made in 1935, while *A Woman's Sorrows* was from 1937, and weren't the shots of Ginza and Shimbashi from that time just wonderful, although the interiors were fantastic too, he said, letting out a sigh, and then said, I think this spaghetti is overdone, and after he'd expressed his reservations about the way the pasta had been cooked, he marked the program according to a system consisting of three types of ballpoint-pen circles—single, double, triple—and passed it to the editor, who cast her eyes over it and said, I wonder if I'll have the time, then said, my salary's much smaller than it used to be, so let's split the meal today, okay?

As far as the woman could see, the editor's statement included at the end of *Tokyo 1934–1993* said *exactly* the same thing about Kineo Kuwabara's photographs as something a middle-aged man she'd had an affair with once had, although according to the MA student, everything that journalists wrote and said was the same anyway. I thought Kuwabara's comments on the photos were interesting, that offhand vague quality they have, he said. About photo number 39 he writes, *It's called* New Year Fair *so it's probably taken at the end of the year*, he said, and laughed, but really, what's with these photos, of course they're not simply inviting people to feel a sense of nostalgia for these past scenes, to think to themselves, like your special feature, "I want to go back to that day," and then he said that the "Nippon Cinema Classics" program certainly didn't evoke a sense of nostalgia, what it presented was unknown, *new* Japanese films, veritable fresh discoveries, but why is it that when looking at photographs where the scenery of some particular instant is frozen in time people succumb to the sensation of being lulled by a sweet nostalgia? Reading this reminded me of the man I used to be with, although those memories are neither nostalgic nor sweet, the woman said, as if talking to herself, in a tone that obviously suggested that she was thinking to herself that her memories of him were not wonderful, but that this in itself was not at all uncommon, then read out loud from the book, *What strikes me most potently is that prewar Tokyo of the 1930s, as we can see from the photographs, was really quite an appealing place that was already equipped everything apart from the technologies we know collectively as electronics, and looking at that place where people interacted so directly with the things around them (even in their poverty) I feel an urgent sense of longing to return to those days*, and that sort of stuff, she said, and the MA student continued, reading aloud the section that said, *Yes, here we see a way of life with an indubitable texture to it: the texture of people living, rejoicing with all their hearts, weeping, letting their noses run, getting dirty, scuffling with one another*, then said, in a slightly pitying tone, was he the kind of person who'd come out with lines like that, and she replied gloomily, yeah, exactly, the kind of person who says stuff like, *We hold within us*

the void, the arid sense of deprivation that comes from knowing
that all that has been lost to us. It is too late. Tokyo will soon be
destroyed. Photography has become the elegy that buries the city
in silver grains of sand, she said, and laughed.

That the scenery gently captured by Kineo Kuwabara looking through the lens of his small 35 mm camera and releasing the shutter induces in its viewers a sense of nostalgia for a city now lost to them should not, naturally, arouse any kind of suspicion in itself. There are people out there, after all, who have seen with their own eyes the exact same streets as those that appear in his photographs, the exact same signs and film posters and white summer hats, parasols of linen and of patterned paper, the imperial court dress that boys wore on the day of the Shichi-Go-San festival, and padded jackets, and aprons, and mongrels with sheepdog blood in them, and dancing girls from the revues with round, stumpy legs like tree trunks, and geisha in their traditional hairstyles, and young girls glimpsed from the back, and women in both kimono and Western clothing passing in front of the billboard with the badly illustrated poster of the Howard Hawks film *Barbary Coast* with their eyes to the ground, and a young apprentice boy on his day off wearing an outfit of striped cotton with a flat cap, and even people who haven't seen those things are still sure to be lured by the sight of that lost scenery into a feeling of sweet nostalgia.

And yet, the staggering number of Kuwabara photographs that so vividly capture these lost scenes and memories of passing moments cannot but bring about a peculiar silence, a peculiar surprise in their viewer. The act of casting their eyes on the great bustle formed by the lives of all the various unknown bystanders in these photographs, all the adults, children, and women who here appear detached from the narratives of their own private lives and histories, which they of course all possess, and yet who seem, in spite of that detachment, as though their lives would not be so difficult to imagine, this all leaves the viewer with a sensation similar to a kind of vertigo.

Looking at the seemingly endless array of photographs showing scenes of common people in which their small moments of joy and varied kinds of despair and loneliness have been gently captured amid the play of light and shadow, we can only gasp in wonder at the scrupulousness of the unfading curiosity that exists in the surreptitious desire of the eye, the finger, and the legs of that person behind the camera who captured them.

But what on earth is with these photographs? A period of sixty years, photographed on the same 35 mm camera, in a mediocre way that couldn't be flatter, even intentionally, as if they were just holiday snapshots or something, so why do these photos draw you in like this, the young man said, and the woman answered, isn't it because the person taking these photos isn't capturing narratives, at which the man looked visibly impressed, as if to say, I'd always thought you were a bit dumb, but you come out with some unexpected things sometimes, and the new editor, slightly irritated, asked, do you write film or book reviews, if they're good enough then we might be able to publish them in our magazine.

Needless to say, people cannot really lose themselves in sweet nostalgia for a bygone era by looking at Kineo

Kuwabara's photographs. Here, in the photographs collected in this book, owing to the nature of the reality that we find among the fleeting, delicately trembling folds that make up the sixty-year expanse of time, or put another way, the creative consciousness of the person behind the camera (who has never before undergone such a highbrow analysis), the easy pace of the feet together with the placid sensuality and supremely personal curiosity directed at a particular momentary scene are able, through the medium of the camera, to surreptitiously, and ever so gently, peel off a thin layer from light's time, thereby gently, reticently, attesting to the immediacy of that light. Light's time, which has had its thin surface layer peeled off so delicately by the camera, not only shows us the distant past of a prewar and postwar Tokyo now lost to us, but also, even in the pictures of everyday scenes from the 1990s, fills that surface with a pale, fleeting clarity.

Chapter Eight – Mild Vertigo

IN WHAT WAS something of a rare occurrence, her husband came home drunk past two in the morning, and, apparently incapable of unlocking the front door, rang the doorbell repeatedly, waking Natsumi up and forcing her out of bed, and as soon as she'd opened the door, he sat down in the cramped vestibule to the apartment and slurred in a gravelly voice, you're not going to go breaking up with me out of the blue, are you, fixing her with his gaze, the very kind of look for which, afterward, she would think that that expression "fixing someone with your gaze" had been devised. She didn't have the faintest idea of what might have gone on, but he couldn't handle his booze well to begin with, and was the type to fall asleep immediately when he passed a certain point of drunkenness, and because her father hadn't been much of a drinker either, she wasn't at all used to being around drunk men, although she'd known a few women who'd get pretty sloshed, but she was annoyed at having been woken up and wasn't in the mood for any of this nonsense, and as she was standing there, silent and sour-faced in her surprise and displeasure, her husband stretched himself out on the floor of the hall, legs and arms akimbo, and began to snore, and initially, because this was a first for Natsumi, she was overcome with astonishment and outrage, but when those feelings had passed she began to get mad, and thought about leaving him to sleep splayed out there in the hall by the door, but it struck her that this wouldn't be a very adult thing to do, and above anything else, her surprise had left her a little nervous, so she shook him awake roughly, saying, come on, pull yourself together, forcing him to get up, somehow managing to get his coat off, but removing his shirt and his trousers from his heavy, half-asleep drunken body proved impossible, so she took off his tie, took out his wallet from the back pocket of his pants (she was always telling him not to put it in his back pocket in case it got stolen, but he didn't listen), and somehow managed to get him into bed, but on top of the annoyance that came from being awoken after two (when she'd looked at the clock in the living room it'd read 2:35) by the noise of the doorbell being rung in that agitated way, at such an insistent speed, ding-dong ding-dong ding-dong, and then having to tend to a drunk person, there was the matter of the outrageous snoring and the breath that stank of alcohol emanating from the bed next to hers, the noise and the stench bothered her so much that she couldn't sleep, then there was what he'd been saying in that slurred, sloppy way, you're not going to go breaking up with me out of the blue are you, the question of what that actually meant, was he really thinking that I'd get so angry with him for coming home plastered that I'd file for divorce, because that's a totally ridiculous train of thought, even for a drunk person, and as she was thinking ir-ritably about how she should act toward him tomorrow when he woke up, she began to feel quite awake, and as a result, didn't get back to sleep for ages, and just as she finally managed to fall asleep and started dreaming she was woken by her alarm.

It was Saturday, and when the children came back at just

after noon her husband was still asleep, and when he did get up about an hour later, the kids said, urrghh, Dad, you smell funny, and her husband lifted up the arm of his shirt as if to smell himself, wrinkling his nose, saying weakly, even my sweat smells like booze, my head and my stomach both hurt, and he took some antacids, chugged two or three glasses of water in a row, had a long bath and then changed into his pajamas, and it still seemed like he wasn't doing great, so Natsumi mixed some of the honey that she'd bought at the agricultural university fair—harvested by the beekeeping enthusiasts in the boxing club—into cold milk and egg yolk to make egg-nog, which she knew from experience was good for curing hangovers, and her husband drank that and then got back into bed, emerging again blearily toward the evening, his hair all rumpled after falling into bed with it still wet, and drawled through a yawn, ahhhh I slept so well, and the kids who were watching anime on TV said, wow, Dad, you've slept so much, and her husband agreed sheepishly, patting their heads, I have, but I'm feeling much better, and then added slyly, and as proof of that, I'm finally feeling hungry, and when Natsumi said, I haven't started making dinner yet, he said, in that case, how about we go out to eat, and the children clapped their hands and said exuberantly, yesss, hooray, can we have tempura, can we have yakiniku, and Natsumi remembered how her stomach had been on those occasions—although there hadn't been so many of them—when she herself had been out drinking with her friends until late at night (usually when one of them had broken up with a boyfriend and was feeling either depressed or jubilant) and had been hungover, when they'd started the night in a small bar without a karaoke machine, drinking all kinds of drinks, like bourbon with water and gin and tonics and Bloody Marys, and Natsumi, who didn't think of herself as being able to drink much, was ordering tequila-based margaritas with a large lemon wedge adorning the rim of the glass, and by the time she waved her hand toward the waiter to order her third, she was already pretty far gone, and everyone said, oh here she goes again, because around that time it was a habit of Natsumi's to explain that the margarita was a cocktail made by mixing tequila with lime juice and pouring the mix into a glass with salt on the rim, which had been devised for young women in Mexico nightclubs who wanted to enjoy drinking like everybody else but weren't good with strong liquor, and was given its name because the white ring of salt around the rim looked like a daisy—"margarita" in Spanish—and at that point someone suggested that it would be cheaper to just buy a bottle of liquor between them, so she'd ended up drinking whisky with water, and she didn't remember exactly how many she'd had, but she was pretty drunk, and ended up staying the night, along with everyone else, at Setchan's place, who by that point had already left home and was working part-time in an architecture firm in Yashio while studying architecture in graduate school, and renting her own apartment near Ichigaya with a six-mat and a three-mat room as well as a kitchen, bath, and toilet for the very cheap price of 35,000 yen a month, and when she'd woken up in the morning and said her head hurt and she felt sick, Setchan had taken a bottle of Pocari Sweat out of the fridge, saying that it was good for hangovers, but the flavor of it, sour and salty and faintly sweet, had reminded Natsumi of the taste of the margaritas the night before and made her burp, and she didn't feel like drinking it, and all of the girls had slept in T-shirts and pajamas loaned from Setchan without taking off their makeup, so they all looked gray faced, and lounged around saying listlessly that maybe they should get up and wash but none of them feeling like moving, and they didn't

136

have any appetite, and in the afternoon they talked about going out to the soba restaurant nearby for something to eat but it was closed on Sundays, and by that point Momoko and Setchan were both very hungry, and started saying how much they'd been looking forward to eating soba in curry sauce, how they'd had a real craving for tempura soba, while Natsumi and Yukari were doing their best to hold back their nausea, and Yukari, who'd just split up with a critic whom she'd been seeing, who was married with children (and as far as they could work out was a very unpleasant, morally lax kind of a man), had given back the T-shirt and pajamas and towel that she'd used, saying, sorry this'll mean more washing for you, to which Setchan had replied, oh no I won't wash them again, you've only worn them for one night! are you that dirty? assuming a look of surprise as she spoke, and Yukari, who had specialized in modern literature and was then working as an assistant in the Japanese literature department of the university she and Natsumi had graduated from, hadn't replied, and, as she and Natsumi were walking along side by side, she blurted out, apropos of nothing, I'm thinking about having an arranged marriage, which she hadn't said the previous night, and remembering that, Natsumi also thought about the arranged marriage itself, and how things with the critic had dragged on even after the wedding, how Yukari had ended up getting divorced, and to this day hadn't been able to break things off with the critic, but that was a whole other problem, back when Matsumoto had been working as an editor, Momoko and Natsumi had said they wouldn't commission someone like *him* to write for them, at which Matsumoto had looked at them with an expression that said, how very childish, and said, if someone writes well then as an editor I'm going to commission them to write for me, that's what the job's about, she'd said, exhaling a puff of smoke from her menthol cigarette, and Yukari, being Yukari, had played the academic, saying how highly she thought of his writing, and so Momoko and Natsumi had felt disenchanted, and now she remembered very clearly how on that day, when she'd heard Momoko and Setchan talking about wanting to eat curry noodles and soba with tempura, it had given her a rush of nausea, and so she said, yakiniku and tempura are probably out of the question for your dad when he's like this, when you drink too much your stomach feels bad and greasy foods can be tricky, she said to the kids, but her husband said, it's okay, that eggnog seems to have done the trick, as long as I have that cold pine nut soup to start I think I'll be alright, and so the kids said, hooray, go Dad, that's the spirit, and got very excited.

It was after they'd got back from dinner, read the morning and evening papers, and were watching the ten o'clock news on TV while the kids were in the bath that her husband said, I found out, Saeki's got divorced. Saeki had been in the same year at university as her husband, changing direction after graduating to become a freelance photographer, and Natsumi had visited his place and they'd had him and his wife Junko over enough times that, even if she wasn't exactly friends with her, she knew Junko relatively well, she was a quiet, reserved type, who could have passed for a beauty if she'd spruced herself up a bit more, made a little more effort, but as it was, she would leave her darkish, lustrous skin free of makeup, and dressed in hand-me-down shirts and sweaters and jeans that had belonged to her husband, who was a sharp dresser, the couple had no kids and she looked younger than her age, and her particular brand of lack of affectation had seemed at first unusual and fresh to Natsumi, and reflecting on it, perhaps the fact that her husband, Saeki, was a fashion photographer and was therefore used to seeing beautiful people dressed to the nines as part of his work meant that he found something attractive in Junko's unfussy, gamine, barefaced style, or at least that's what Natsumi would sometimes think.

Huh, really, but they always seemed to get along so well, Natsumi said in surprise, to which her husband replied, it definitely looked that way from the outside, Junko did everything for his business from answering the phone to the accounts, and when he was feeling dissatisfied with his work and went to Africa for a few months she didn't complain even once, and when he got involved with his models she turned a blind eye, I always thought she was either the perfect example of "the wise and hardworking wife" that people often talk about, or else, a little bit obtuse, he said with a sigh, and then went on to explain that she had started out working in the accounting department, and had been in charge of the accounts at Saeki's office, so she was very used to that side of things, and apparently she'd spotted a promising-looking opening in *Travail*, that women's recruitment magazine, and had found a new position for herself a year ago. In other words, she'd got everything prepared, found a job, and then went through with her plan. She must have been waiting for the perfect opportunity. When Saeki got back home after being away for work for a few days, he thought the place looked strangely empty, and there was no sign of Junko, or their four cats, and then he realized the reason the place looked so out of the ordinary was that most of the furniture had disappeared, but still he thought that she must have just decided to redecorate, albeit in a slightly extreme way, figuring she probably put the old furniture in storage somewhere, or else sold it before the new stuff was supposed to arrive, that was what came to mind initially, although it was still a bit odd, for sure—you remember, right, their place was hardly crammed with furniture and objects to begin with, it always had a minimalist feel—but he decided that for the time being he'd have a beer, and when he went to the kitchen he saw that the sideboard where they kept the dinnerware was gone, and laid out on the counter by the sink was the pan that he'd used when he was living alone to cook instant ramen, along with a kettle and a frying pan, and a few plates and a broken rice cooker, and the gas stove and the fridge were still there, but all the other kitchenware, the pans and everything else were gone, and as he was trembling in shock, trying to understand what on earth had happened, he opened the fridge—apparently it was empty except for three cans of beer—and he sat down in the living room, where the only piece of furniture left was the sofa, and was drinking the beer when she came in through the door. And she said to him, I've started renting a new apartment and I've moved in, I've found a new job and I start work next week, half of our savings are in my name anyway, but I paid off the deposit with the money that I got from refunding your commuter pass, there's no point trying to persuade me, I want you to sign the divorce papers, all this in a tone of unshakable resolve, and when Saeki begged her to tell him why she was leaving, she simply kept saying, this is the decision I've made, and wouldn't say anything else, and when he said, I admit I've made mistakes in the past, can we please just talk things over, she stayed silent, and when he asked what had happened to the cats, she'd said that all four of them were well and living happily in her new apartment so he had no cause for concern, she'd found Mopé and Yukimama herself so it stood to reason she'd take them with her, and when, losing control of himself, he'd shouted, well if you look at it like that, Tom was a cat that I found myself, so leave me Tom, Junko had replied, Tom was a kitten that Yukimama fed and brought up side by side with

Yuki, he's friends with all the others and it wouldn't be right to leave him on his own, to which Saeki had pleaded, in that case let me have both Tom and Yuki, and Junko had thought for a while before saying, well, to be perfectly honest with you, I'm fonder of Yukimama and Mopé anyway, so I don't mind, and the following morning she brought back the two cats (a fat white one and a tabby with white paws and belly, spayed and neutered respectively), which at least was a silver lining for Saeki, he loves those cats so much, anyway, all of this happened a month ago, and in the end he signed the divorce papers and sent them off yesterday, and that was why we were drinking, it came as a real shock, her husband said, and then continued, Junko's already forty, so she's got guts, I guess you have to give her that, but it feels like her way of doing things is a bit under-handed or something, he said falling deep into thought.

Hmmmmm Natsumi said, also thinking the matter over, and what she thought was that she didn't know Junko very well, but there was some inscrutable quality to her, you never re-ally knew what she was thinking, which made it seem quite plausible that she might go about things like this, and after-ward, it struck her that you could only do this sort of thing if you didn't have kids, and so she said to her husband, that's the kind of thing you can only do when you don't have kids, isn't it, to which her husband said, well, maybe that's true, but does that mean the bond between childless couples is really so delicate and flimsy, sounding like he was parroting something he'd read somewhere, or delivering a line on a cheesy TV show, and so Natsumi responded by saying, well, that's love for you!

Sometime afterward, Natsumi received a phone call from Junko, now divorced, informing her of her situation in a very matter-of-fact tone. Natsumi, concealing the fact that she'd heard about the divorce from her husband, said, that must have been exhausting, which made Junko laugh and say, you're the first person to say that to me, that it must have been exhausting, most people when I tell them that I've gotten divorced say things like, oh that must have been terrible, still, you're ever so brave, and so on, to which Natsumi said, but I'm right aren't I, you're exhausted I'm sure, just thinking about it all, I can imagine how tiring it must be, mentally and physically, I don't think it's something that people who resent exertion would be able to manage, and Junko said, hmm, you're right, it was tiring to a certain extent, but with us—I imagine that you've already heard his side of the story—it wasn't a case of another man or woman, no falling madly in love with other people or anything like that, so the emotional dimension was phenomenally easy, it was just the moving house and everything else that was a little tiring, she said, leaving Natsumi at a loss for how to reply, or what to think, and so, for the time being, she adopted the persona of a housewife who knows little of the ways of the world, saying in a somewhat overblown manner, really, gosh, that's so admirable of you, and as she said it, she thought about how it was kind of odd to use the expression "with us" when talking about your divorce, and afterward, she said to her husband, that's obviously not something you'd say if you were referring to yourself alone, but surely divorce is about breaking apart that "us" and going out into the world as an individual, of course it's not a big deal or anything, but I feel like in this case she could've at least said, "with him and me," or something like that, to which her husband replied, whichever way you say it, though, she was the one who walked out on him, I can't see that the nuances of her word choice really matter in this situation, and don't give me that naive stuff about establishing herself as an individual and all that, what I can't get over is the fastidiousness of how she did it, it's like that battle cry—"fast as the wind, quiet as the forest, daring as fire, immovable as mountains"—that's what surprises me, if people have to get divorced then they have to get divorced, he went on, I mean in the case of Yasuda and Yokobori it couldn't be helped, right, even if we did meet at their wedding party, he said, and then remarked, in a tone suggesting he was deeply moved by what he was saying, one couple separates, another one gets together, but still, Junko's ... and there he broke off, apparently speechless.

There's nothing admirable about it, though. That's the thing, she went on, in a cheerful voice, a tone of voice with bounce and luster to it, I feel really fulfilled, I told an aunt of mine who I'm close to—she's a tanka poet, as it happens—about the divorce, and on those sorts of occasions, most people say things like, oh that's terrible, what are you going to do now, and so on, they look at you with a pitying expression, you know, but this aunt of mine is different, she's always been that way, that's just her nature, and she listened to what I had to say, and replied, I see, just those two words, and then do you know what she said next, she said, now you must go and have a fabulous romance. Isn't that wonderful? Ever since I decided on the divorce, I hadn't cried once, not even the very last time we talked—he was crying, though—but when she said that to me, it brought tears to my eyes, I mean, don't you think it's just wonderful, to say something like that to a divorced woman of forty? It cheered me up so much, made me feel a lot braver, as if I do have a future ahead of me, that love and life are lying in wait for me, that's honestly how I feel now. Really? Natsumi said, to which Junko said, when I find a boyfriend I'll introduce you, and giggled, and put the phone down.

There are people like that, aren't there, Natsumi said on the phone to Matsumoto when she rang her up to tell her about it, and Matsumoto gave a contemptuous, ha-haah, then said, wow, that's really something isn't it, saying that to a forty-year-old woman, "a fabulous romance," hahaha! And she's a tanka poet, she said? how perfectly romantic, to which Natsumi said, but you know, she might well end up finding a boyfriend, that's how it is with love, ever since it was first invented there've been people who go around saying, oh but when it comes to love you just never know what'll happen, thereby robbing people of any possible response, Natsumi said, to which Matsumoto said, that's not what I'm saying, though, I'm talking about the phrase "a fabulous romance," it's so *conceptual* sounding, so abstract, that woman sounds pretty dumb, she said irritably, if you ask me, most people who write tanka are left-wing nymphomaniacs, and if I'm not allowed to say that, then they're *definitely* all hyperromantic, passionate types, I can't stand them, she said, and then added, I've got to go to the tennis club, trying to end the conversation and put the phone down, but when Natsumi said, oh, have you started playing tennis, she replied, I don't know how long I'll keep it up, but I've put on a bit of weight recently, I'm getting out of shape, why don't you come along sometime, so Natsumi said, noncommittally, yeah maybe, and Matsumoto said, okay byeee, and hung up, and so Natsumi changed the children's bedsheets, put the dirty ones in the washing machine, and polished the kitchen sink with a metal scourer into which she'd squeezed some cleaning fluid.

The slightly sticky pink foam spread across the surface of the sink, and the fine wire of the scourer cut into her fingers with a sharp pricking sensation, which was a regular occurrence and wasn't something she paid any attention to, and it was always after she'd started using the metal scourer and her hands were already wet that she would think, oh yes, I should've put dishwashing gloves on, but by then she didn't want to waste her time drying her wet hands with a towel and putting on gloves, and so she'd just continue as she was, gloveless. When she turned on the tap to rinse away the pink cleaning fluid, she found herself gazing at the water that was falling from the tap like a twisted rope, forming a small whirlpool by the drain before it was sucked down and away, gazing at it and succumbing to a faint stupor. When she'd finished cleaning the sink, and went to fill the kettle, intending to make a cup of tea, the same thing happened again, and although the water was spilling over from the top of the kettle, she found herself simply staring at it, as if she were being drawn into its momentum, and while she was standing there, incapable of turning off the tap, she grew dizzy and her head began to spin, she had the feeling that she'd been there for quite a while like that, but of course in reality it was only thirty seconds or so, and she snapped back to herself and turned off the tap, tipped away some of the water from the kettle, placed it on the stove, and lit the gas.

Do you ever find when you're in the middle of doing something that you zone out and suddenly find yourself becoming a bit dizzy, she tried asking her husband, who said, that probably means you're getting a bit anemic, come on, let's have a look, he said, pulling down the skin beneath her eye like kids often did when they were making silly faces and taking a look, saying, you're okay, yeah, you're okay, your blood is properly red, then saying, your face looks funny like that, you remind me of something, I can't think what, and he cocked his head in thought, which seemed to Natsumi somehow very juvenile, and it irritated her.

That Saeki, her husband said, as if the thought had just randomly popped into his head, he's a real rogue, he seemed in such shock when Junko left, and was saying how this time he'd really change his ways, but it turns out he's already living with another woman, so Natsumi said, oh really, and then muttered under her breath, he's having a fabulous romance, and her husband said, hmm, what's that?

The woman Saeki was marrying this time was a stylist for a company that produced mail-order catalogs whom he'd met through his work after Junko left, and when he'd complained about the lonesome widower's existence he was leading with his two cats (a large white one, and a black-and-white tabby that someone had abandoned, both neutered), and their sad culinary habits, with the cats subsisting on dried and canned food, and him eating out all the time, she'd said, in a very casual, offhand way, that she adored cats but her landlord who lived downstairs hated them, and was a real stickler when it came to hygiene, so she couldn't have any of her own, and she loved cooking to the point that she'd attended culinary school and gotten her chef's license, and whenever friends of hers had gotten married she'd always done the catering for their wedding parties so it really wasn't a hassle, why didn't she go over and cook for him every once in a while, and so Saeki had replied, without any lecherous intent or hidden agenda, that it would be a real help, and after this arrangement had carried on for some time, their relationship had developed, her husband explained, and because it had come about like this they weren't going to have a ceremony or anything like that, but had instead decided to invite just their close friends and have a party at home, to which, her husband said, they'd been invited, but on the day itself the younger boy came down with a fever, and Natsumi had been unable to go, so she still hadn't met the person who was now known as Saeki's wife.

She hadn't heard any news of Junko having found a new

man after leaving home, she hadn't in fact heard anything from her at all, and the fact that Junko had said on the phone that she'd send a postcard with her new address but no such postcard had arrived bugged her, she still had Junko's copy of *All About Knitting: The Basics, Vol. I*, which she'd borrowed, not to mention the expensive umbrella with its orange fruit and white flower print that Junko had left one time when she came over and they'd agreed that either Junko would pick it up or Natsumi would bring it the next time they saw each other, and leaving the knitting book aside—she might open it up if she began to knit again—the wooden-handled cotton umbrella, although some would surely have argued that its lifelike pattern of green leaves, brown branches, orange fruits, and white flowers against a blue background would brighten one's mood on a gloomy rainy day, wasn't at all to her taste and she wasn't very inclined to use it, so it sat there untouched in the umbrella stand by the door until, on her way back from seeing the cherry blossoms in the Equestrian Park, Setchan had popped over to take measurements for the new desks they were going to have made to order from someone they knew for the boys, the younger one who was about to start elementary school and the older who had been making do all this time with his dad's old desk, with chunks of its legs chopped off to shorten it, it had started raining just as she had left, and so Natsumi had given her the umbrella to protect her from the downpour, and Setchan, after seeing the pattern of the umbrella, had gone off singing *the hill of my memories/where the mikan flowers blooooooom/by the blue sea*, with the "blooooooom" part sung out of tune.

Unlike when the younger boy had been in kindergarten, she didn't have to make a lunch box for him to take in every day, and also didn't have to cross the road to drop him off and pick him up from the agricultural university in time for the school bus because he now went in with his older brother to the local public elementary school, which made things much easier for her, and of the kids who'd been in the final year at Aoba Kindergarten, quite a few had entered private schools, and even of those who didn't, many were in different districts meaning there were only four kids from his year in kindergarten at the same school, which came as something of a relief when she remembered what the mothers there were like, and considering all that, she did have the feeling that now was the time when she really should think about doing something, maybe getting a part-time job, but when she consulted Setchan and Matsumoto about it, they brushed her inquiries away quite brusquely, as if to say, what would a career woman like me know about finding work for a housewife of nearly forty with no career to speak of, no résumé, it's really not my field of expertise, I wouldn't even know where to begin, what exactly is it that you're asking of me, and maybe it was only natural for them to respond that way but it infuriated her nonetheless, and she remembered how in the fall of the previous year, when she'd read the essay by the novelist on the Kineo Kuwabara exhibition that Setchan had copied for her, she'd phoned up Momoko and explained to her how the women in the essay were so much like Setchan and Matsumoto, and the pair of them had laughed about it, so she'd said to Setchan in response, you know those essays you gave me, I thought it was funny how the women in them were so much like you and Matsumoto, to which Setchan had replied, did you think so? well, I guess that's the way it goes, and laughed, and then the tone of her voice changed slightly and she said, if I were a housewife and I weren't in a situation where I absolutely needed to earn more money there's no way you'd find me working, I'd lie around being blissfully bored, I'm the type who's always hated going out to work, I'd much rather stay put at home, she said, in a tone of voice that underlined her earnestness, and Natsumi thought about how, when she encountered the full-figured housewives in the food section of the department stores who were so obviously part-timers, and who would say to her with a conspiratorial wink, oh, don't go with that one, you don't want that, this one's much tastier, pointing her toward the pickles or deep-fried food at which-ever stand she was working at, gently steering her choices in a "just between us housewives" kind of way, Natsumi would think, hmm, this is something that I could do, and would then wonder if, actually, generating this sense of trust and famil-iarity established through their both being housewives was actually a technique straight out of the sales manual, and she found that she was just as busy as ever without really being able to say what occupied her days, and all that formless time sliced up into sections slipped past before she knew it, and as soon as they entered June it transpired that her mother had to go into the hospital to have surgery on her cataracts, and the surgery itself wasn't major, but her mother rang up to ask if she'd take care of her father while she was in the hospital, saying, I wish I'd gotten him used to doing at least a little bit of the house-work by himself, showing him how to do things always feels like such a bother and I get so irritated and end up thinking that I'd rather just do it myself, but times like these make me think that people really should have their husbands do things around the house, I mean this for you as well, you should do it while you still can, and after stating that opinion, she went on to say, I'm sorry to ask this, but would you mind coming to Mejiro for a few days, even if it's just at lunchtime?

When she arrived at her parents' house in Mejiro, after stop-ping at the Shimo-ochiai hospital to check in on her mother, her father said, I know your mother was worried about me, but I can manage all by myself, I can use the microwave, and back in my student days I made pork and sweet potato soup for everyone in a settlement house in Yamaya, so I don't know what all the fuss is about, when you and your brother were born and your mother went into the hospital, I managed just fine by myself, he said, dredging up experiences from some thirty odd years ago, and that night, when she ended up staying over at Mejiro—her husband and children went out for dinner at a new Chinese restaurant that had opened in their area—her father said to her, you should treat this as a day off as well, I don't expect you to cook, why don't we order in sushi or something, but thinking that sushi alone wasn't nutritionally sufficient, Natsumi prepared a dish of simmered young potatoes, cabbage, and carrots with peas and deep-fried tofu, and soup with finely shredded kelp, and after their meal that they'd eaten in front of the TV, interspersed by short bursts of pointless conversation, her father got up and took a square envelope out of one of the drawers in the living room dresser and said, we found this photograph among your Yukigaya grandma's things, your mother said she was planning to give it to you, and Natsumi replied, what photograph, this is the first I've heard of it, and looking at the black-and-white photograph smaller than a postcard she saw, although she had no memory of the occasion, her own self wearing a sleeveless white dress with tiny red polka dots, which had been made for her when she was in the second year of kindergarten, and when she'd started school the following year she'd suddenly grown taller and bigger, and so even when they let out the hem of that dress that her grandmother had made for her the previous summer, the waist was a couple of inches too high and looked absurd, the sleeve holes were too tight, and she remembered that her mother had said, as if surprised, this is what they mean when they talk about kids shooting up like summer grass, so she knew immediately that she must've been in her second year of kindergarten in that photo, which had been taken under the jujube tree in the Yukigaya garden, a straw mat laid out on the ground on which she and her brother—who was still more or less a baby—were sleeping, and their Yukigaya uncle, who was wearing a straw hat and sitting with arms folded in a wicker chair placed slightly away from them, had a faint smile floating around his mouth as he looked toward the camera, while Natsumi was sleeping peacefully beside her brother and the toy bear—which had belonged to her Yukigaya uncle since he was a child—and the white cat Mimi with different-colored eyes, she didn't remember the photo being taken at all, and her father said, I wondered why your grandmother didn't give it to us, a photo like this, with a look of puzzlement on his face, and then continued, out of the blue, we asked her to come and live here but she wouldn't, so we offered to move to Yukigaya but she wouldn't agree to that either, she insisted on living by herself, she was a strong-willed woman, and then he noted that it was twenty years since she'd died, which gave Natsumi a very peculiar feeling. The next day after lunch she stopped by the hospital again, and in the afternoon, walked around Mejiro for the first time in what seemed like forever. Outside the secondhand bookshop on Mejiro-dōri was a rack of paperbacks on sale for 150 yen, and she'd paused in front of the bookstore for some reason, perhaps because she'd developed a faint desire to read something since seeing her father, after dinner the previous evening, lie down on the sofa and take out a detective novel—at least she imagined that's what it was— saying, I feel bad doing this while you're here, I know you don't come that often, but I want to find out what happens next, and Natsumi hadn't heard of either Edna O'Brien or Iris Murdoch, but the cover illustrations were kind of approachable—which was really to say, were the kind of crass illustrations by female illustrators that you saw in women's magazines that had something perfectly *novelistic* about them—so she picked them up and read the descriptions on their back covers.

One of them read, *"In the past, I always felt that whether I went toward him or away from him I was only doing his will. But it was all an illusion." The illegal immigrants, scholars, high-ranking bureaucrats, and ravishing diplomat's daughters making up this fabulistic world all find themselves in thrall to the mysterious enchanter, Mischa Fox, with one brown eye and one blue,* and speaking of eyes that were different colors, her Yukigaya uncle's cat had had eyes that were green and blue respectively, a big, white longhaired cat that was apparently part Persian—she couldn't remember which eye was blue and which was green, but the green one could also take on a golden-brown hue depending on the light—and her uncle had said that because of something to do with their genes, cats with different-colored eyes were often deaf, but his cat didn't seem to be, and that's what the book's blurb made her recall although it was really entirely unrelated, and the back of the other book read, *Separated from her heavy-handed husband, Nora falls into the arms of a succession of men. Yet if their embraces bring her physical satisfaction, they leave her spiritually empty. Plagued by a sense of unfulfillment, she becomes acquainted with Hart, a close friend of her son's, and the two begin a passionate affair. In the midst of their lovemaking, however, sudden disaster looms . . .* and she thought that falling passionately in love with your son's best friend was certainly, however you looked at it, incest of some sort, and that made her think back to when she'd been living in the Mejiro apartment, and the man living upstairs in the biggest apartment in the building was a cultural attaché from Switzerland—in reality she didn't really know what he did for work, but it seemed as though he was doing something related to film—while his wife Masako wrote poetry (she published her own pamphlets) and their blond sixteen-year-old son went to boarding school in Switzerland and even though Natsumi had only seen him once, she thought he was an extremely attractive boy, who didn't at all take after his bald father who reeked of cologne and had a moronic air about him, and of course didn't look like his mother either, and Masako had once said to Natsumi, when I think about him I get this sensation that I'm pretty sure I wouldn't have with a daughter, I feel my blood stirring, that's how it actually feels as his mother, she said with a degree of candidness that made the truth of what she was saying impossible to doubt, it was even quite startling, and of course Natsumi didn't experience it as something she "actually felt," but she could see that it was likely an incontrovertible fact that some women out there in the world really did love their own sons hopelessly and unconditionally, yet when she considered her mother's attitude toward her brother and her mother-in-law's toward her husband, she couldn't see any sign of that type of hopeless devotion, it then occurred to her that maybe her grandmother had been that way with her Yukigaya uncle, but leaving that aside, as far as she could tell from reading the blurb on the back cover, it was obvious that this kind of story line would culminate in a disaster of some kind, and yet she also had an impulse to read just this kind of turbulent, romantic novel that veered so wildly from reality for once, and in any case, the books were all 150 yen, which meant they were less than half price, so even if she got bored and abandoned them midway it wouldn't be such a great loss, and so decided to buy them both.

Outside Mejiro Station, she bought beef for frying in butter, roast ham, and bacon—which was on sale—and some of the doughnuts filled with azuki bean paste and mochi wrapped in kashiwa leaves that the kids liked from the Shimura confectionery store, figuring that if she bought vegetables and milk there in Mejiro she'd be weighed down on the journey back, instead resolving to buy them from the supermarket near her apartment on the way home, and in a newly opened café she ordered a coffee and a slice of carrot cake, and took out the paper bag containing the books from her handbag, but when she opened one up and flipped through the pages she didn't feel particularly inspired to begin reading, the carrot cake was fairly tasty, not too rich, and she was quite keen on the unfussy ambience of the café that reminded her of a log cabin, but in a crowded café like that it was hard to concentrate for even a couple of pages on a passionate affair or mysterious enchanters or heavy-handed husbands or spiritual emptiness that endured despite sexual satisfaction, and so she decided to take her time reading the books at home instead. She had a feeling that she'd encountered a story line with a woman who fell desperately in love with her son's best friend either in a TV series (a Japanese one, of course) or in a book, or had it been the story of a woman who got involved with her son's friend after losing her son, and suffered greatly as a result, in any case, it seemed there were an improbably high number of women out there who nurtured this desire to have sex with some transfiguration of their own narcissism, and with that thought, holding her bag containing her shopping, she picked up the bill on the table, paid it, and left the café, only to find the young man who'd been reading a magazine at the next table come running out after her, saying something to her. Dressed in a cheap pink polo shirt and jeans, the boy had a kind of unsophisticated air, so she imagined he was a university student who'd come to Tokyo from the provinces and was living by himself in a small apartment, and with an earnest look he said, here, this, and held out a book, and when Natsumi looked at him in puzzlement, he said, I think you left it on your table. Ah, so it's not like he had any particular desire to speak to me after all, she thought, as she said, oh, thank you, I'm not used to having a book with me so it's easy to forget, I'm getting old and senile you know, this last comment half in earnest and half expecting him to protest with an expression that said, c'mon, that's not true, but the boy nodded gravely, and said, I sometimes leave my books on the luggage rack in the train, so Natsumi widened her eyes and said, that must cost you a fortune, and the boy laughed and said, I don't do it all the time. In any case, the two of us have both just had a coffee, so it's not like he's going to invite me to have another one, Natsumi thought to herself, with a little flicker of disappointment, so she took the book, thanked him again, said, I just bought it and I haven't read it yet so I'm pleased to have it back, and smiled, and the boy said goodbye, turned around, and went back into the café.

The episode wasn't a big deal of course, not in the slightest, but it did go to prove how genuinely rare an event it was for a housewife to speak to any man other than her husband, Natsumi thought to herself on the train from Mejiro to Shinjuku, the only other men that she really encountered were the super of her building (if you could count someone that old as a man) and the man who would drive up in his truck to sell produce direct from the growers, who wore a white headband and whose skin was tanned very dark (who'd said to one of the local wives, probably only meaning to be nice, why don't I take you out sometime, eh, and the local wife had laughed and said, feeling flush are you, in that case you can take me out to Roppongi, but the expression "feeling flush" had apparently rubbed him the wrong way and he'd replied, hardly, I sell at such giveaway prices I barely make a profit at all, and the local wife had replied, what are you talking about, do you think I haven't heard of small profits and quick returns?), and the door to their apartment building wouldn't open without entering a security code, which meant she didn't have salesmen knocking at her door, and both her sons' homeroom teachers at elementary school were women who'd been teaching for decades, and the hairdresser at her usual salon was a woman, and of course she hadn't met with her old male friends at all since she'd gotten married, and it had never occurred to her to miss those interactions, or think the loss of those friendships a pity or anything of the sort, but when she stopped to think about it, it seemed to her that when the women with the types of professions featured in the glossy pages of women's magazines who looked far younger than they actually were said how they wanted to remain attractive and stimulating as women however old they got, what they were really suggesting is that they wanted to continue to be sexually desirable, but in her case, just as how when she had been a young girl she'd been viewed in that way whether she'd been conscious of it or not, now, she wasn't even conscious of the fact that she was being treated as a sexless middle-aged woman, she was contemplating these things as she walked briskly down the underground passage joining the Yamanote Line platform and the Odakyu Line platform swarming with people coming and going in all directions and boarded an empty car of the Odakyu Line train that was waiting on the platform, rested her brown imitation-leather shopping bag that had grown surprisingly heavy on her lap, and let out a sigh. And really, it wasn't a big deal at all, but it was quite bizarre when you thought about it, now the upbeat, slightly accented voice coming over the speakers announced that the train would be leaving shortly, warning people of the closing doors, and then there was the hiss of the air escaping as the doors shut and the metallic scrape of the wheels starting to move along the rails, and she thought to herself, wasn't it actually quite an extraordinary thing, when both the Iris Murdoch and the Edna O'Brien books—although she hadn't even started either of them—were ostensibly dramatic adventures in which romance played a defining role and, on top of that, seemed to be exploring religious morality and the meaning of existence, why then were the world of the romance novel and the reality she inhabited so far apart, suddenly that fact, which was of course nothing at all to wonder at, was absolutely to be expected, seemed to her for a moment quite peculiar, quite strange, and when she thought that she would doubtless carry on living this kind of uneventful life with no opportunities to meet any men other than her husband, in a permanent state of tedium, the words "mm, that figures" formed on her lips, as if it were not in fact her own life that she was thinking about but someone else's, and four high school boys diagonally across from her—two of whom were standing, leaning forward holding on to the leather straps, and two of whom were sitting down—were talking in loud voices, yeah she wouldn't stop calling me and I was getting sick of it so I agreed to go out with her, but then in the café she was all like, do you love me, she kept asking me, and I was like, what's that got to do with me, so I didn't say anything, and she suddenly gets mad and is like, you're in love with Naomi aren't you, out of nowhere, so I was like, what the hell's that got to do with anything, and she frowns and storms out, and it's like shut up, just shut up will you, leave me alone, you can't just call me up like that out of nowhere, like what the hell, you know, girls man, I'm telling you, they're a pain, they don't leave you alone, and they want all this stuff from you, you're better off renting videos than putting up with that, it's way less hassle, I'm done man, I've had it with girls, they moan all the time, we haven't even *done* anything and already it's like I love you I hate you and all that shit, it's way better to find a good video with a girl who's your type, on and on they went, and to Natsumi's right were three women in their sixties in mourning attire, all wearing black jackets over black dresses with pearl necklaces and talking about how the chikuwa fish sausage made by Kibun was disgusting, and their voices began to blend together. What day is your collection day for oversized garbage? Oh, we have to pay for it where I live, last year when I moved in with my son and his wife and their two kids, they said that they'd gotten rid of a lot of their stuff and so in the end I threw away so many of my possessions, I could hardly go on saying that I thought it was a waste, oh yes of course, there's not all that much space for either of you, and he knew full well he'd have to strip down to his pants for the examination but he still came in those gross old man briefs, I wanna say to him like, if you're so clever then what the hell are you doing in a school like ours, it's only Kawamoto and Sasaki, and when I said to my mom I wanna buy boxers so give me 5,000 yen she was like, why are you spending so much on underwear, you're not going to go and buy anything kinky are you, and he was my son's colleague when he was over in Britain, and as a gift when the baby was born he gave them something he'd worn when he was a baby—this absolutely wonderful garment with the most elaborate smocking, although it had yellowed a little over time—as a gift you know, isn't it marvelous to have kept your old clothes like that, but you know, that's because they have big houses over there, with attics and cellars and so on, yes of course, and the telephone bill came to 38,000 yen, my dad was just fuming, going like, why is it this much, that's crazy expensive, honestly Nomura's like, when he calls me he doesn't really talk and just says whatever it is he has to say, but when I ring him he goes on and on about all this unimportant crap, talking about his girlfriend, you know he's got a girlfriend right, like she did this and she did that, and when I'm like, I'm gonna hang up, he'll be like, come on, you can stay on a bit longer can't you, it's always like that, even so, 38,000 yen is like …, no but it adds up, I'm telling you, anyway shut up! you sound like my dad, honestly, it does happen, when the wife starts going to work, well you know what people are like these days, as soon as their children are old enough they're out of the house again, they're all dying to get back to work, it's different from how it was in our day, they're getting their own incomes, my younger brother lives in Chiba, his wife started working, started earning so much she bought a brand-new car, and now when she goes out to work in the morning she refuses to give her husband a lift, saying he'll get her car dirty, so he drives the older one himself, I wanna get more muscly, I don't wanna end up looking too bulked up or anything but it's not cool to be so scrawny, all puny like Kawamoto and Sasaki, you look way better in uniform if you've got a bit of muscle, like around here, are you gonna get ripped like Muki-Muki Man, no way, not that much, I'm not gonna overdo it, I just want my clothes to look good on me, so the high schoolers and the sixty-year-old women went on speaking in high-pitched voices, and Natsumi thought that tonight she wouldn't make sukiyaki after all, but spaghetti bolognese instead, and as she pictured the contents of her cupboard and her fridge, she figured out what she needed to buy in the supermarket, canned tomatoes, parsley, basil, powdered cheese, and spaghetti, and then, like usual, she started visualizing how the supermarket looked inside, how she would go in and, across the aisle from the vegetable section immediately to her left-hand side containing salad and green vegetables, root vegetables, tomatoes, and cucumbers were the

159

fruit, the mushrooms, and the dairy products, at the back was a Kinokuniya bookstore and a Pasco bakery, and next to that was the deli counter selling ham, sausages, and Western-style cold cuts, beside that a glass case containing tempura, cutlets, and croquettes, to the right-hand side were the milk and dairy beverages, kitchen products like frying pans, pots, and grilling racks, cloths, garbage bags, aluminum foil, Saran Wrap and so on, and across the aisle the various kinds of cleaning products, bleaches, and fabric softeners, for the kitchen, bathroom, toilet, laundry, and the rest of the house, cutlery, paper napkins, and paper cups, plastic containers in assorted shapes and sizes for storing food, ladles and corkscrews and can openers and kitchen knives individually packaged with a cardboard back and see-through plastic front and arranged neatly in rows, numerous varieties of instant ramen and cup noodles and cereals in brightly colored packets, and sometimes in the refrigerated display case of the fresh fish section there would be assorted kinds of expensive fish laid out on top of the stainless steel racks, but it was on Tuesdays that she went there, because that was Fish Special day, which meant the cases were lined with polystyrene trays of tuna or red snapper or yellowtail or octopus sashimi or whatever else was on special that day, and on the shelves alongside it there were always shijimi clams and Japanese littlenecks and Asian hard clams and fresh seaweed in packets, and next to them, in polystyrene trays sealed with film, were tuna chunks and tuna scrape, boiled octopus, rolled omelets, broiled eel, cod roe, squid, surf clam meat, not to mention raw squid, lightly salted cod, Alaska pollock, fresh salmon fillets, rosefish fillets, sardines, horse mackerel, small horse mackerel for deep-frying, smelt for deep-frying, scallops for cooking with, steamed scallops, and scabbard-fish fillets, and in the frozen fish display case alongside were several kinds of black tiger prawns sorted by size, large Japanese tiger prawns, peeled shrimp, shelled Japanese littlenecks, ground whitefish meat, frozen mixed seafood, and scallops, and in the meat section beside it, polystyrene trays containing semi-prepared cutlets, yakitori, diced steak on bamboo skewers, meat-stuffed cabbage rolls, hamburger patties, chicken, ground beef, ground pork (with a label reading Guaranteed 80% Lean Meat!), mixed ground meat, and packs containing thin slices and thicker cuts of loin, thigh, and belly meat of imported beef, domestic beef, wagyū beef, black pork, and Specific Pathogen–Free pork, and packs of meat especially for frying in butter and grilling on a hot plate and for making sukiyaki and shabu-shabu, and in the beef display case were the slightly more luxurious cuts of tongue and steak and sliced beef for sukiyaki and joints for roasting, and on the shelves beside that were a huge quantity of ready-made curry roux, various kinds of seasonings, Chinese and ethnic ingredients, ready-made rice porridge in packets, and all kinds of seasonings to mix in when cooking rice, and across the aisle were the soy sauce and other sauces, expensive imported balsamic vinegar and olive oil and wine vinegar, Bovril, anchovy sauce, all the different kinds of miso paste, all the different kinds of salt, picturing it all half-unconsciously, and then as she was remembering that she'd bought beef for frying in butter, but thinking that she could always put it in the food processor to make ground beef, she started feeling faintly nauseous, and her field of vision began to sway slightly in a way that was different from the vibrations of the train, as if she were experiencing a kind of mild vertigo.

Afterword

INTERIOR DECOR

Oh you're right, Sofia was saying, she told me not to change the sheets, the cleaning lady would do it, that's what she called her, "the cleaning lady," Sofia said to K. now, with a look on her face like she could not believe it. The friends were in the fluorescent-lit green room upstairs at the Strand, which also appeared to double as the employee break room, as they were waiting to have a conversation about Sofia's new book in front of about twenty people, a disappointing number, but it had just started to rain, and also the bookstore charged a $7 cover, much to K.'s irritation. The two friends hadn't seen each other in person since the previous spring, when Sofia had taken the train in to the city, this time to appear for one of K.'s events, but they continued the conversation they'd been having over email all that month of October, when as chance would have it they were both guests in multimillion-dollar brownstones for some period of time, Sofia at the home of a childhood friend in D.C. to record her audiobook, and then staying there the night before her trip to New York. K. had somehow found herself ensconced with her family for more than two weeks in the dimly lit basement studio apartment of a brownstone near her older daughter's school, at the grace of a former graduate student, who lived there, on the top three floors, with her husband and child. This was due to a series of calamities that occurred in succession that fall, including her toddler testing high for lead exposure, which triggered a series of visits from the health department, and finally their landlord being forced to carry out lead abatement, rebuilding and repainting the walls, doors, and baseboards. Upon returning earlier that week it was uncanny being back in their apartment, the bright-white walls and doors, made of a cheaper material, often retrofitted over the existing scuffed and chipped surfaces, the pillows on the gray couch now looked so faded and ugly, all of their stuff had been moved back, during an exhausting eight-hour day that Monday, her usual day off from teaching, assisted by a team of movers, although nothing was on the wall, no children's drawings, or her husband's small paintings, none of the touches that make a place feel lived in, and they couldn't find many of their things. How could this home be so beautiful, Sofia had written to her friend in something like a panic earlier in the month, while staying as a guest in her friend's house, why don't I possess this art of living, everything is clean and cozy, wherever you look. As K. had now inhabited the interiors of rich people's houses this year, for playdates with children from her daughter's school, and having been a guest in the basement level of this modernist renovation, sometimes creeping upstairs into the light, she assured Sofia that the answer to all this was just money, rich people hired interior decorators, they outsource childcare, they don't have to work full-time or even part-time, they all call themselves artists, K. had written, but they don't have to produce much because of a lack of financial exigency, it drives me insane! It can't only be money, Sofia had responded, possibly defending her other friend, yes they do have a lot of money, but you must care about your home, about the arrangements of your home, you must clean constantly—and I would just rather wallow in filth and discomfort on my slovenly couch. K. had assured Sofia that her friend absolutely without question hired someone else to clean her house, maybe twice a week even, the rich just hide it, they hide everything, and now in their conversation in the ersatz green room she was of course proven right, she couldn't even feel smug about it. But I don't understand how they find out about these things, Sofia had written in their earlier exchange, to which K. responded, fast, They spend their days on Instagram! Everyone has the same exact things! She knew from this constant research, re-searching their research, the exact cost of the ubiquitous dove-gray status ceramics she was served on playdates. If I went on Instagram for a second I would kill myself, Sofia had replied, which ended the conversation for a while, the petty conversa-tion running underneath other conversations, to be picked up again, when they saw each other.

All of this longing toward perfect objects and interiors re-minded K. of *Mild Vertigo*, the 1997 novel by the Japanese writer Mieko Kanai, which the two friends had spoken to each other about for years, largely speculating on its contents by what they could gather online, before it had been translated from the Japanese, by Polly Barton, for which K. was supposed to write something for the New Directions edition. Though she was expressly asked not to share it with anyone, she immediately forwarded the Word file to Sofia in September, so that they could read it together, so that it was inhabiting both of them, during the time of this exchange. The narrator, a housewife named Natsumi, also regards other people's apartments with something like an investigatory gaze, as gleaned from catalogs, including knowledge of the Ginori 1735 teacup with a fruit pat-tern that she's served tea out of by the childless and wealthier married neighbor, in the second section of the novel, which is divided into eight sections with each part structured around a conversational encounter, and was originally published in installments in a women's magazine. While living in that unfamiliar basement studio apartment beneath the brownstone, on her days off from teaching when the toddler napped on the bed next to her, K. had tried to read the printout of the translation that the publisher had sent, although she found it difficult to focus, and soon her daughters had scattered the pages all over the heritage quilt, which was actually extremely cozy, as was the bed, much more comfortable than theirs at home, which was about fifteen years old, their white duvet so yellowed and shabby her husband was too ashamed to bring it along for their stay—it all felt in some way like they were temporarily living at one of those extended-stay hotels for traveling businessmen, because of the chaotic nature of the interior decor and the rather sterile setting, in such sharp juxtaposition to the curated light-filled spaces upstairs they entered rarely. Where does someone buy sheets that don't cost a fortune? Sofia had wondered to her in that same earlier thread, and K. sent her a link to the Amazon-brand organic sheets she had purchased when they had subletters in August, along with new towels, nothing fancy but fine, she had written. The shame we feel over our dirty houses, she wrote to Sofia then, it's class shame, when the movers came and took all our furniture away and I could see the cloudlike gatherings of dust bunnies under the girls' beds, the horrible guilt and shame I felt, at my dirty house, at my daughter's lead poisoning, I try to sweep, but I'm too busy to do anything more than pick up toys and trash and wet towels and pajamas off the floor morning and night, I run around like a crazy person picking everything up. In *Mild Vertigo*, the wealthy neighbor complains to Natsumi that her home is a mess, but the narrator observes critically that it looks like a showroom, impossible for her own home, with her two small children, where everything is always in chaos. As the two friends sat there at the bookstore, talking aimlessly, both of them extremely tired and overworked, K. from childcare and teaching the past week, as well as moving back in, and Sofia from the long train ride after a morning of classes, along with the demands and exhaustion of that first week of a publicity cycle, K. wondered whether she knew Sofia well enough to discreetly wiggle out of her tights in front of her and put them in her backpack, but decided against it. The Wolford tights that she found in the back of her closet, which she must have purchased before having her children, or at least before having her last baby, pinched at her waist, as did the control-top underwear—she only wore undergarments like this when doing an event and while wearing a dress—and K. had tried to steam her black silk dress for an hour in the shower, underneath she wore her one black nursing bra that her husband assured her passed the sniff test, all of the wilted black clothes that had lived rolled up in her suitcase for weeks while they had to be out of the apartment. She was probably so bloated because she was finishing up a heavy period, still crampy and bleeding lightly on a medium pad, one of her first periods since having the now two-year-old, the pad that she checked, in the employee toilet, before going on, although it had been since before being pregnant that she had been able to spend any time or money taking care of her body, had thought much about her body at all. They take so much care with their health, Sofia had written to K., in wonder at this alien species. Not only yoga, she continued, they swim every day, they eat superfoods I've never heard of, they look amazing, they will never die, Sofia had written her in her hilariously fuming way. Well, everyone dies, K. had written reassuringly in reply, although as usual enjoying Sofia's resentment and irritation. You too would be good at life if you had any time, K. assured her friend then, if you had leisure, if you had money. But K. understood this irritation too—the parent-child class at her eldest daughter's school where she had taken her toddler that morning was full of beautiful women with long shiny hair and glowing beautiful skin, and, like Natsumi's gossipy neighbor, they wore the most impeccable casual wear, earth-toned matching knit sets for both themselves and their beautiful children. Many lived in the multimillion-dollar brownstones, which formerly contained several apartments but were converted into bespoke single-family homes, displacing artists and families of color over the previous decade, a fact that K. was only now realizing, finding out the addresses through Zillow, StreetEasy, or Realtor searches and researching buildings' histories, a new hobby of gently simmering rage. The moms would sit on the tiny wooden chairs made by Quakers and eat the warm rolls kneaded at the beginning of class by their drippy-nose toddlers, and talk about how it was all so hard, while their nannies waited with strollers outside, and everyone brought knitting to keep them busy as they watched their children play together with the handmade knitted animals and wooden toys, except K., who wrote books and had no talent, patience, or time for crafts, so she also sat, helping fold the cloth napkins, in a class that was so calm and happy but left her with a clawing and weeping sensation in her chest, as she wore her toddler in the carrier to the station, where they would take a shuttle and then transfer to another train home. Maybe this weeping sensation was because of the cognitive dissonance of their wealth, and the resulting class irritation, despair, and occasional rage that had been omnipresent, all fall, since the lead poisoning situation and then more recently when her kindergartner was diagnosed with a mouthful of cavities on her first dental appointment since the pandemic. Oh, I wish there was a way I could write about all of this in my essay, K. said to her friend, now the next afternoon in the lobby of the art deco West Village hotel that Sofia's publisher had put her up in, as they sat on the velvet couch in front of the fireplace, which reminded K. of the orange velvet conversation-pit-style couch sectional downstairs, on the other side of the studio apartment's back door in the brownstone, where her family occasionally hung out basking in the light flowing into the space from the two-story wall of back windows, while the other family was at their weekend farmhouse, but that she stopped venturing up to, to the light and coziness, preferring instead the sterile dimness of the basement, with the Japanese paper on the only two front windows, and the dismal gray-brown flooring always warm from the thrumming of the building's mechanical room in the subbasement below, but still with the luxury fixtures like the chrome-handled sliding closets and warming toilet and combination bidet. Kanai Mieko parodies all this, she now said to Sofia—as they sat there on the red velvet couch, everything overwarm because of the fire—the constant worry over the clean house, it opens with the narrator moving into the new modern apartment complex, with a separate kitchen, her mother's voice layered over hers, at the impossibility of getting their former kitchen clean, at the worry and shame of a dirty kitchen making someone appear impoverished, connecting to her parents' working-class roots, the worry of the interiors seen in the pages of women's magazines an uncanny corollary to the internet now. It makes me think of my mother in our small suburban house, K. now said to Sofia, and how there would be no broom or dustpan, just like in this house I was staying in, we couldn't find it, the idea is that one was just supposed to not make a mess, or if they did, to pick up the crumbs off the floor on one's hands and knees. I don't want to make it personal, she said now to Sofia, I'm bored of writing these essays about books where I put my autobiography inside, I definitely don't want to write about the teeth or the lead, but how else, to show the interior of an experience of a novel like this, how a novel invades you, as much as you invade it? The two writers began to talk about their husbands, who do most of the cooking at home, unlike Natsumi, who is afraid to cook fried food because she doesn't want to get the kitchen messy, although she wasn't a talented housewife who takes pride in bringing in homemade snacks to the kindergarten, like the others, yes, they were lucky that their husbands did the cooking, but what about organizing time, making appointments, following a calendar? K. told Sofia about the black Moleskine planner she kept on trying to fill out all fall, trying to find a way to schedule appointments despite her overstuffed teaching schedule and constant conferences with students, the now weekly dental appointments, the flu shot clinic at the pediatrician, the next round of bloodwork, let alone when she would even have time to read the entire book and write an essay about it, although she had in many ways already spent the money. That September she had negotiated up to $1,500 from $1,000, because she knew that none of them had been to the dentist since the pandemic, and that the fashionable pediatric dentist in Park Slope, which gave children balloons and tokens for plastic baubles out of machines, was $375 with X-rays, and as it would turn out, the $1,500 would pay for only part of the dental work her daughter needed done, which would take regular visits throughout the fall, as explained in emails about the updated treatment plan, with reference to a diagram of a mouth, with red Xs indicating all the cavities, and the silver-capped tooth and its twin, the L and K, had already cost $800. All of these calculations were constant inside K., and she and her friend complained to each other about these men in their kitchens, and how impossible it felt to get them to take on the organizing, the mental load. But what was the reverse, to do it entirely alone? Divorce is a specter in *Mild Vertigo*, Natsumi needs her husband to complain to, they occupy that bubble together, despite her isolation, despite him never really validating her feelings, which causes the perpetual prick of irritation, he is one of the only people she has to talk to, besides passive-aggressive mothers and the occasional social outing with unmarried intellectual friends, as in the penultimate section, "Female Friends," which incorporates a review of a photography exhibit, possibly written by the author, in the form of a photocopied handout given to Natsumi, a conceptual trick that reminded K. of Lynne Tillman's Madame Realism persona. Occasionally K. notices Sofia looking at K.'s waist, sitting there on the couch, and she wondered if she noticed the high-waisted wool trousers that she had recently bought, despite not being able to afford them, for the events that she would be doing that month, wool trousers are a practical purchase, thinks Natsumi in the novel, and perhaps what she should do with her mother's offer of a little retail therapy, or a practical bag to carry, or even a new appliance or something for the children, but instead she is talked into a tea-colored Missoni silk blouse, with which she has nothing to wear, she wears it to a fancy restaurant out with her single girlfriends, who are all dressed too casually, perhaps even she needs to find a job, outside of the house, in order to wear this silk blouse that brings her such ambivalence and yet also pleasure. Sofia always looks pretty and stylish, for the reading she was wearing an elaborately embroidered coat, she always looks like herself, K. thought, she doesn't need fancy designer items to feel like herself, if Sofia knew how much K. had spent on these trousers, she would feel horrified, K. was certain, although the trousers had the right hang and bagginess, and almost all of her other trousers were still too snug after having the second baby, it's really better when she was standing up, you couldn't see it when she was sitting down. The two friends begin walking, anxiously following the digital directions on their phones, through downtown Manhattan, to the ramen place where K.'s husband and the little girls would meet them, past young people lined up outside of the pop-up Halloween costume store, they kept on getting lost, crossing the street. It was one of the first times that K. had been inside a restaurant for years, and the first time they'd been out to this ramen place since before the children were born, her daughter's mouth was still sore from having her cavities dug out of her molars that week. Sofia had gifts of pocket-size kaleidoscopes for the girls that twisted a blue-tinted stained glass, always knowing the perfect things to get her children, K. thought. Feeling celebratory, K. ordered warm sake for the adults (it was the cheapest house sake), which they drank out of tiny cups, deliberating on levels of spiciness, tonkatsu or vegetarian broth, tofu or chicken, soft eggs or none. The children shared broth and noodles and chicken out of two colorful plastic bowls, the toddler picking up the long noodles and stuffing them in her face, soft food was still good for the still-sore mouth of her eldest—they were so well-behaved and happy to be there that K. felt such love and warmth toward them, watching them. She noticed that her older daughter's face looked slightly uneven, although her husband said he couldn't see it. She sat there and watched her child's lovely, swollen, uneven face, and somehow sensed with the ambient and constant feeling of dread that this meant her mouth was infected, that there would be antibiotics and even more dental work in the weeks ahead, in fact she would soon learn that the silver-capped molar would have to be extracted, but for that moment she allowed them all to feel pleasure, being with each other, seeing their friend. The next week Sofia sent her older daughter an envelope filled with two tiny blank books she made from a leftover calendar, as well as a charming drawing in colored pencils of her small house.

MILD VERTIGO

One Sunday morning, having woken up with the clocks one hour earlier because of daylight saving time, feeling that vertiginous, dizzying feeling, perhaps because of being overly warm, it was another mysterious and somewhat disturbing 70-degree day in November, K. began to try to work on her notes for her essay she was supposed to write on *Mild Vertigo*. She lazed around mostly braless, the underside of her breasts hot and sticking, her armpits stinky, with underwear she kept on changing, and sometimes a robe, with the sash her almost six-year-old, who hadn't yet had her extraction, kept stealing to use as a jump rope, with a distracting thumping sound. She thought about how much the narrator in the novel changed her sweaty underwear when inside the apartment, or philosophized about her PMS, how radical that felt, for this other type of bodily realism to appear in the space of a novel. The day before, that Saturday, she had been to the park near the school, resplendent with yellow leaves, for a birthday party for her daughter's schoolmate, and she was feeling worn out from all of the socializing, as well as from attempting to paper over with a smile all the constant pricks of class irritation she now felt, living in Brooklyn. I need to be able to complain to you of my class resentment, she yelled out at her husband, in the other room. Like when that mom told me I was a supermom because I don't have my toddler in day care, as if we could even afford it. She felt slightly sunburnt and depleted, and her daughter complained of her stomach hurting, possibly from the three chocolate cupcakes from the day before, of course she was the one who let her daughter eat as many cupcakes as she wanted at the party, and the sucker from the gift bag, she wondered if that's what these people were thinking, of these parents with the child with the rotten mouth and the other one with lead poisoning, although she did worry about their nutrition, whether they were getting enough iron, calcium, vitamin C, which was what was advised to combat the lead. It's boiling in here, open the windows! I can't think with the heat in here she yells crossly into the other room at her husband, who was getting ready to take the kids on a bike ride and to the playground. K. had decided it was her day off and she was going to sit on the couch and think about *Mild Vertigo*. Are you sure it isn't a hot flash, her husband had said to her, and she pointed at the thermostat, 76 degrees, although she was extremely hot, and dehydrated, overcaffeinated, exhausted, as the two-year-old woke up at what was now 5 a.m., because of the time change. While waiting for the children to come back she sat in the chair by the open front window that she never sits at and watched the gentle swaying of the Halloween spiderwebs in the wind, with the brown crinkly leaves stuck inside, those will have to come down, listening for the chatter of her children coming down the street, as well as the plaintive squeaks of a male cardinal in a bush that for a while resembled a fire alarm with a broken battery, the swaying, swaying, she was stuck there, for a second, just watching, feeling something like a nervous ecstatic feeling, like pent-up energy, which was slightly relieved by going into the other room and masturbating absentmindedly. I don't want to put my life in it, my grocery list, because of all the grocery lists, my messy house, my messy life, my husband I'm perpetually irritated by and feel warm toward, the patter of bickering, she wrote to Sofia that day over email. I wonder if there's some way to replicate the layering of voices, a doubling feel, the novel as interior decor, the novel as apartment block, chapters as spaces stacked next to each other, characters as neighbors, gossiping about them providing the narrative momentum. A narrative like an aviary, how invasive it is, interior, the ventriloquism the novelist performs, cleverly done in the chapter remembering a childhood parakeet with her mother, the chattiness of Natsumi's mother's voice on a phone call. On Google Maps with the help of the New Directions editor K. had located the sprawling residential suburb where the novel is set, the park where the children play, it is near the temple of cats featured in Chris Marker's *Sans Soleil*, which is also an essay on Hitchcock's *Vertigo*, this seems to be referenced in the multiplicity of stray cats and the interludes of intrigue and gossip that they elicit from the cat ladies. In the essay Sofia had written years earlier imagining the contents of Kanai Mieko's novel, published at *The Paris Review*, she intuitively referenced *Sans Soleil*, citing the scene of the Japanese woman sleeping on the train, not knowing yet the mystical ending of the novel, Natsumi zoned out, slightly nauseous, overcome by the vibrations on the train and other voices. How referential the novelist is, especially about film, her next novel after this one named after Godard's *Two or Three Things I Know about Her*, a film which shares a similar modern corporate apartment setting with *Mild*

Vertigo, as well as the narrator-housewife protagonist, and all of the interior design in Godard films, the meditation on late-stage capitalism, even here in *Mild Vertigo* there's a witty digression on housewives so bored they become prostitutes, all of the films of housewives becoming prostitutes that *Mild Vertigo* references: Buñuel's, Godard's, Chantal Akerman's, except here in the novel nothing happens, the tedium is the point, the potatoes are peeled, the dishes are washed, and sometimes, sometimes there is a meditative moment of housekeeping, a dizzy or spaced-out feeling, when washing the dishes, the constant rope of water pouring out of the faucet, hit by the sparkling of the streaming water, that sensation that Polly Barton translates as a "mild vertigo," the title also of the eighth section. Stream of consciousness sounds so easy, like it flows, but there is something more spatial happening here, thoughts filling up the blocks of pages, playing with attribution to conjure a sense of disorientation, like the Bernhard narrator frozen in the wing chair relentlessly pursuing ugly and petty thoughts about the fellow partygoers in *Woodcutters*, the constant calculations, of the apartment layouts, of all of the things needed to be bought to fill up the apartment, all of the things, perhaps Mrs. Dalloway bought the flowers herself but she didn't have to do everything herself, she had to throw a party but not to clean everything, cook everything, buy everything, think about birthday presents, Father's Day gifts, anniversary gifts, the litany of these lists stacking up on the page, the constant worries as a series of digressions, a novel of a constant mental load, the husband is lazing on the couch watching TV, and the housewife's thoughts and memories and anxieties and things to do are never-ending, the sentences are thoughts, a barrage, a constancy, like the things that need to be bought, a buzzing in the head that sometimes resembles the dread patter of a buried middle-aged Beckett housewife or Stephen Sondheim's "Getting Married Today," swallowing received language and parroting it back, parroting other clichés. It was such a good place for the children, the area, their school, their grandparents in the country. As soon as one day was vanquished another sprang up, all of the lists of what to get her little children when they go stay with the grandparents for the summer, like when K. has to ready her oldest to go to school the next morning, to stand outside at the bus stop at an ungodly hour, the two-year-old up again at 5 a.m., K. is the one who has to play drill sergeant, gently rolling her child who wants to curl back to sleep, out of bed, taking her to the bathroom, yanking the brush through her hair, laying out the new purple sweatsuit, now that it is finally cold enough this morning to wear it, where is her purple backpack, is the medicine packed, is the lunch made, saying to her husband, does it have to be a turkey and cheese sandwich every morning, and leftover Halloween candy—what must the teacher think of us, with our child's rotten teeth!—yanking on socks, packing water, washing the toddler's face, coaxing her into a diaper, reading her a book, watching them eat their hard-boiled egg in their little bamboo bowl, Come on! Come on! You have to brush and floss! It's 7 a.m., sneakers on! Yanking on gloves, coats, to her husband, who is silent in the kitchen, Can you please take out the plastic to the recycling, it's scattered everywhere … Every day it will start all over again, this Sisyphean maintenance labor, there is so seldom, as Kanai Mieko writes, a way to "punctuate the monotony of everyday living." In her notes K. wrote that Annie Ernaux's book on suburbs and consumerism is called *Exteriors*, in *Mild Vertigo*, the exteriors are swallowed up, become interiors, like the narrator having totally internalized the layout of the grocery store so much that in a trancelike state at the end she finds herself moving through all of the aisles, reciting all of the offerings at hand. Perhaps she could just make a list of everything K. thought about and worried about, was asked to do or order online, while trying to write this piece over a few days, outside of the usual student emails, publishing emails, landlord emails, doctor and blood-work appointment emails, looking at her husband's shaggy hair and asking him to make an appointment at the bourgeois barbershop, then making it herself for next Saturday, or trying to figure out what to get the neighborhood kid for his sixth birthday without spending more than $10, would a boy like the same hand-painted wooden bead necklaces they've been doing, and why not, two Saturdays from now, RSVP yes for 4, or nagging her husband to fill out the dental insurance form and help her sign the PDF of the teaching contract again for the spring, thinking about birthday and Christmas presents, researching, ordering the cake for her daughter's sixth birthday Thanksgiving weekend, and the cupcakes to bring to school, one has to be vegan for one of the children, better make it all vegan, three dozen mini cupcakes of chocolate-vanilla and vanilla-chocolate and chocolate-chocolate, and thinking about a striped floor pillow for their reading nook, that will make the place look lively, and replacing a melamine plate because her husband stepped on it, and they only had two small plates for the children, first finding the manufacturer and ordering it from them directly, she was out of the special cotton pads for removing her makeup, and (her husband tells her, shouting from the kitchen) dog poop bags, which just arrived as she was writing this, a sad Amazon box with an econopack of unscented dog poop bags, and her daughter tells her she wants a new dress for her birthday, and wondering how to afford that, worried about all of the money they were hemorrhaging, and thinking of getting the children an inexpensive keyboard for

Christmas, and where would they put it, other children have musical instruments in their houses, and emailing the school nurse about her daughter's antibiotics, and filling out the on-line bus schedule, and where were her daughter's one pair of tights in the laundry, were they too dirty to wear for Picture Day this week, the day before the extraction, and what would that do, to attempt to live inside of it, although she was already living inside of it, these spaces layered over each other, the space of the novel, the doubling domestic space.

— KATE ZAMBRENO